Sacrifice

—

Jessica Gadziala

Cover Design by: Jessica Gadziala
Cover image credit: Shutterstock. com/ Jag_CZ

Dedication

To Anne.
Who believed in this even more than I did.

Chapter One

Lenore

The Sacrifice was something spoken of in whispers, lips quivering behind closed doors.

It was the phrase thrown at children to secure good behavior.

Do your studies; You don't want to become The Sacrifice, do you?

Watch your tongue; I don't want you to be the next Sacrifice.

Unfortunately for my mother—and, as it turned out, myself—I had always been a headstrong child. I was a girl with far too many opinions, and far too few inhibitions. I was always running when told to walk, singing when I was told to be silent, proud when I was told to be humble.

See, The Sacrifice was both a verb and a noun.

An action.

And a person.

In this generation, that person was me. That action to be taken was my life would be handed over.

There was nothing to be done.

Nothing my mother could say.

Nothing I could do to prevent it.

The day began before dawn, my door creaking open, a dozen sets of footsteps quietly filing in, trying not to wake me. As if I had been able to sleep the night before. Which was when they'd told me I was the Chosen One. I was to be this generation's Sacrifice.

I only got one night's notice because they didn't want to risk me trying to run off. As it was, our small cottage was surrounded by guards to prevent any temptation to take my chances with the woods I had known as my home my entire life.

Our little village was far away from the ugly outside world, with its superficiality and cruelty.

I would never see this village again.

That was a thought that had plagued my mind the night before as I walked numbly back to my room, dropped down on my bed.

This place, these people, this way of life.

It was all being taken away from me.

I tried to block out the sounds of my mother's muffled weeping in the other room.

The only daughter of an only daughter of an only daughter, our family had been cursed for generations. While other mothers enjoyed three to six little girls pulling at their skirts, sitting at the tables learning the meanings of the cards, the names of the gems, my mother had only me.

And now she was losing me.

My heart ached for her.

But it raced for myself.

Because no one knew what happened to the Sacrifice once she was handed over. Assumptions ran rampant, of course, as they would in any small community. The more creative of the girls invented tales to be told around a campfire, like normal children might do with ghost stories.

Except there was a very good chance that these stories might be real.

That I might be stripped bare and gang-raped every day for the next few decades.

That I might be strung up and bled dry slowly over time.

That I might be cut to bits and eaten piece by piece while I was still alive.

No one knew.

The not knowing was the worst part.

I had no idea what to mentally prepare myself for.

I suddenly wished I had been a better student, that I had sat quietly and let my mind drift away for hours during meditation. Had I applied myself, I might have become one of the star pupils, one of the young women who could endure beatings during meditation without feeling a thing. I could have been one of the Transcendent Ones, meant to be one of the leaders of the coven.

I could have avoided this all together if I had been a better daughter, a better student, a better member of our community.

It was too late to change now, though.

As I heard the women's hushed whispers beginning a chant I had seen in our family grimoire on the table in the living space, something I had pored over at the table when I was younger—so curious about darker things, convinced there was no way they could ever happen to me, I could feel my empty stomach churning.

I knew this was it.

It was the end.

I had so naively thought I had so much life left to live, so much more to experience.

Now, it was all being taken from me.

The chanting grew louder as the moments passed, meant—I imagined—to gently wake me.

As if sleep was ever possible for the Sacrifice.

As I lay there, I suddenly remembered the tale of Avia, a supposed Sacrifice from eighty years past, who had learned of her situation, and had convinced one of the guards to sneak her a handful of the belladonna hidden in the Poison Garden, allowing her to end her life before she had to be Sacrificed.

She'd saved herself.

And damned another young woman who had done no wrong.

And to be fair, Avia had done wrong.

Just as I had done.

Over and over.

Year after year.

If I took the coward's route and took my life, who would take my place?

Maeve, whose biggest misstep in life was once falling asleep during an all-night moon circle?

No.

I couldn't force my fate on her.

So I stayed in my bed.

I let my thoughts swirl.

I waited for the rituals to start.

Hands grabbed my covers, drawing them down my body, exposing my white muslin nightdress, allowing the early morning chill to penetrate through the thin fabric, causing gooseflesh to prickle up over my skin.

"It's time," Marianne, our High Priestess, told me, sensing my alertness even though I kept my eyes shut.

Taking a deep breath, I made my eyelids flutter open, finding Marianne standing above me with a candle glowing in a glass jar in her hand, setting her face in light and shadows—her sharp cheekbones, her square jaw, her moss-green eyes. Her silver-streaked red hair was pulled into the elaborate braided style that was standard for our coven, both for beauty and for practicality.

They ushered me out of bed and the house, into the common circle in the yard where we would sit at night and talk, where we would perform rituals, where we would celebrate the solstices.

A tub had been pulled into the center, the water full of herbs and flowers, smelling earthy and comforting as my nightdress was stripped away and I was pressed into the water.

The warmth of the scented water eased the tight muscles in my neck and back as the women walked in a clockwise circle around the tub, chanting.

They chanted for my safety.

For my protection.

For my peace.

My eyelids fluttered closed as I started following their chants inside my own head, feeling a calm start to wash over me.

It wouldn't last, of course.

Because, too soon, I was pulled out of the tub, the chilly morning air whipping my wet body as two sets of hands set to drying my skin and hair.

A small twinge of insecurity made my belly swirl. Nudity was something natural in our community of all women. Full moon rituals involved stripping off our clothes to bathe our bodies in moonlight.

But the last time hands were all over my body was when I had my first blood cycle at thirteen. I remembered feeling this same insecurity as they bathed me, dressed me, and welcomed me into womanhood.

Dried, they wrapped me in the pure white gown and cloak, both embroidered with a pentagram between the shoulder blades, that were saved for The Sacrifice.

Finally, I was pressed down into a seat as my mother moved out of the crowd, giving me a sad smile as she moved behind me, combing out my hair then working to plait it into ornate braids as the other women started a new chant.

Not for my peace.

Not for my protection.

But a chant about the gift of the Sacrifice, about her holy place in our coven.

My jaw tightened as I cast my eyes down, not wanting to show them my resentment.

It was easy for them to chant about the gift of the Sacrifice, about my holy place. When they weren't the ones going off to some unknown, horrible fate.

My mother's hands kept moving from my hair to my shoulders, giving them a reassuring squeeze. Each time, tears swam in my eyes, making me squeeze my eyelids tight, fighting them back.

I didn't want to cry.

I didn't want to beg to stay.

If I was the Chosen One, I wanted to go with some dignity intact.

I imagined there would be plenty of time for crying and begging for mercy in my future.

And, I reminded myself, my place *was* important.

If not for the Sacrifice, the treaty would be voided. And that meant the women of my coven would be free game to the whims of their evil souls.

I wasn't sure how accurate the tales were, if the truth could survive thousands of years, but the story we were told was that in the time before the Sacrifice, the coven had been constantly under attack. Women and girls had gone missing, never to be seen again, fates unknown, and there was very little that could be done by the coven to protect themselves.

When dark times came, witches were always targets for small men who were afraid of our power.

The Sacrifice gave us peace to practice, to live free of the ill intentions at the hands of men.

And, I guess, if you looked at the situation as a whole, it was a fair trade.

One woman.

To save dozens more.

I would be doing this to save my mother, to save the little girls with their bright smiles and carefree laughter, even to save my peers who had always been better community members than I had been.

I was the least useful member of the coven.

I was expendable.

My pride might have hurt with that realization, but there was no denying its truth.

And there was no stopping my fate.

Once my hair was braided, the sun was casting golden fingertips across the sky, and the small girls were walking into the circle dressed all in white, carrying hand-woven baskets brimming with flowers they each took turns placing in my hair, their soft little voices humming a lullaby we had all been sung as babes.

When they were finished, they each took a turn standing in front of me, clasping their hands in prayer position and pressing them against the top and centermost parts of their forehead where I had—and they would eventually have—a dark blue crescent moon tattoo: the symbol of our goddess—the pointy tips disappearing into my hairline.

I opened my eyes for them, taking in their innocent faces, reminding myself that I was saving them from terrible fates.

It was a salve over my resentment.

Because I knew that, should some man with ill intentions break into our paradise, I would throw myself in front of each one of them to save them.

This was no different.

It was simply far less dramatic.

A noble Sacrifice.

That was what I could be.

"Lenore," Marianne said, voice deep and firm as it often was when she addressed me. "It is time."

My heart darted around in my chest—a rabbit in the gaze of a predator—but I nodded to her as I reached for my mother's hands, giving them one last squeeze, offering her a smile I didn't feel, then falling into step behind Marianne.

We made our way through the woods in silence.

Marianne and I had never been close. On a good day, I never knew what to say to her.

Today was not a good day.

We reached the road an hour later, finding a single black van waiting, the back doors thrown open. The driver was nothing but the back of a head obscured by a hat.

My stomach flip-flopped as Marianne walked me to the van, climbed inside, then reached to help me in as well.

My gaze fell on the box there.

Pine wood.

Plain.

A line of air holes drilled into the top.

A coffin, of sorts.

My gaze skittered to Marianne, finding nothing on her face that betrayed her true feelings.

But that was the way of the High Priestess.

It was about the coven, not herself.

And, in a way, I finally understood what that meant.

Marianne pulled open the lid, revealing nothing but the inside but a strong wooden box.

Taking a deep breath, I stepped inside, lowering myself down into the space, folding my arms over my chest, and watching as Marianne lowered the lid.

The hammering came next, nails into place, trapping me in my coffin prison.

Doors slammed.

The van lurched to life.

And I was off to become a Sacrifice.

Come what may.

Chapter Two

Lycus

"This fucking rain," Ace grumbled, waving a hand out at the window where the yard was steadily forming pools of water after five full days of nonstop, unrelenting rain. The wet was seeping in through the house's stone, making all the fabrics inside start to feel damp, chilling all of us through.

We'd been around for longer than any of us cared to count anymore, but not a single one of us had gotten used to the cold and wet. It went against our nature.

What can I say? We spent most of our immortal lives in a very warm climate.

We all missed it.

Especially on days like this.

Ace—all six-foot-four of him—was pacing along the wall of windows. Dressed all in black, he looked paler than usual, something that made his red-flecked ice blue eyes even more dominant a feature. His blond hair was messier than he was typically known for, proof of the weather wearing on him.

"Have a drink," Drex suggested, already holding a glass of whiskey in his hand at two in the afternoon. The answer to everything, in Drex's opinion, was to have a drink.

Unlike Ace, if you came across Drex on the street, you would place him as the biker that he was. Six-two, wide-shouldered, and dark-haired, he was dressed in worn black jeans, a wrinkled white tee, and a leather jacket. His beard was a prominent feature of his face, obscuring the bone structure we'd all been looking at for generations. He also had blue eyes, but a darker, stormier color than Ace, with only a small fleck of red that looked like a small birthmark in his iris.

"I don't want a drink. I want this shit to stop," Ace grumbled, pausing his pacing to stare at the relentless rain for another moment. "Sounds like Seven is back," he said a moment later.

And over the pounding of the rain hitting the roof, I could hear the rumble of Seven's bike coming down the road that led to the house.

Maybe normal people would worry about his safety, riding on a bike in the rain.

But we weren't normal.

We weren't even people.

And since we couldn't die, there was no reason to worry about anything.

The engine cut, and a moment later, the front door groaned open and slammed shut before Seven's footsteps came down the hall, and into the front room where we were situated.

Seven was tall, but more solidly built and dark-skinned, with his long black hair loc'd. His dark brown eyes had a starburst of red from the pupil, making them look on fire, something that always made people take a step back from him.

"Fucking crazy," Seven said, shaking his head as he shrugged out of his dripping leather jacket.

"The rain?" Ace asked.

"Yeah, but only because everything is clear."

"What do you mean everything is clear?" Ace asked, glancing over at him.

"I mean I was driving for over an hour. It's only raining here."

"In this town?" Drex clarified.

"On this street," Seven told him, shaking his head.

Ace slowly turned from the window, looking over at me, brows pinched.

"Do you think it's her?" he asked me.

"Her who?" Seven asked, having been out of town when the shipment came in.

"The new witch," Drex said, having been the one to pick her up several days before.

"It's that time again?" Seven asked, shrugging.

"The other one has been gone for years," Ace reminded him.

"Years, days, it's hard to keep track," Seven said, moving over to get himself a drink. "How would it be her?"

"Remember the one, what, three generations ago? When she got pissed, she set shit on fire," Drex recalled, likely because his very own jacket was once set on fire. While he wore it.

"So, what?" I asked. "This one is sad?" I asked, rolling my eyes.

"You know how they are," Ace said, and I wasn't sure if he meant witches, women, or humans in general. In all cases, I figured he had a point.

"Someone should go talk to her. Has anyone even let her out?" Seven asked.

"Minos has been feeding her," Ace said, shrugging.

"For how long?" Seven pressed.

"I don't know. A week? Something like that," Drex said, waving it off.

"Maybe someone should go talk to her," Seven suggested.

"What?" I asked when Ace's gaze fell once again on me. "Me? You want *me* to go talk to her? Why the fuck me?"

I couldn't be considered the softest touch of all of us. If anything, I was probably the worst with human interactions in general.

"Send Minos. Even Seven would be a better choice." Drex always needed to be left out of interactions with humans if it required anything resembling diplomacy.

"I need her to stop making it fucking rain," Ace snapped, "not assure her everything is going to be alright."

"So you want me to scare her?" I clarified.

"Whatever it takes. I don't give a shit. Just make it stop," Ace demanded, storming out of the room.

Once upon a time, Ace had been in charge of all of us. Which was why, when we decided to create the MC a hundred or so years before, Ace had stepped into the role of president without any of us questioning it.

So when he issued an order, he expected it followed through.

"You're going to want a drink first," Drex insisted, holding out a glass toward me.

He was right.

I did.

So I took it.

Threw it back.

Then moved to stand.

We always kept the witches in the basement. At least at first. We'd learned early on that giving them too much freedom at the beginning only created minor disasters. Things being broken. Spells being cast. Jackets lit on fire.

We took them from the van and into the basement, leaving them there for a few months or a few years until their spirits broke enough to allow for them to do what was needed.

There wasn't much to be said about the space. It was a massive, cold part of the house where the damo seeped in through the cinderblock walls, chilling you through to the bone if you stayed for more than a few moments.

We'd thrown shit down there to keep the witches from losing their minds. A bed with a passably comfortable mattress, a couple lights, extra blankets.

Ace, a lover of books, a collector of new editions, tossed all the old ones into boxes and put them in the basement for the witches to read. There was a sink and a toilet. Though I was pretty sure we forgot to add in a shower. Someone suggested it—likely Seven or Minos—but then no one had ever called someone in to work on it between the new arrivals.

It had been at least three witches since I stepped foot in the basement.

I guess I hadn't been prepared to find it any different.

What I found, instead, was that the witches had slowly but surely over time started to make the space more like a home.

Dried flowers were strung and hung from the ceiling. If I remembered correctly, the witches always did some ridiculous ceremony for their 'Sacrifice' in which they filled their hair with flowers. From the looks of things, these flowers had donned the heads of at least six witches. I wondered which one found them all and set to making the place more their own.

The walls, which I remember being painted white after there was some mold issue or another that fucked with the lungs of one of the witches, were suddenly stained in intricate murals. Flowers and trees and woodland creatures. Then, in a break in the woods, a massive pentacle and a couple of rune symbols that I recognized, but didn't know the meanings of.

In front of that pentacle image, someone had set up what appeared to be a makeshift altar.

There was an old broken stoneware bowl that I remembered from one of the many remodels over the years set with various rocks, some worn soft from the river bed that skirted the inside of the woods around the property, and a bushel of dried herbs from the yard, bound with twine. There were feathers gathered in a drinking glass—bright red Cardinal, massive brown and white hawk, a shining black raven. There was even a collection of animal bones stacked in a neat pile, likely remnants of dinner from one of the owls around the property.

We had taken them away from their coven, but clearly not their practice.

Which was why I was here in the first place, I reminded myself, forcing my gaze away from the altar, stepping over the tray of food left at the bottom of the steps to be taken back up. Everything was gone save for the slivers of chicken.

Fucking witches and their refusal to eat meat.

"Hey, where are you?" I called, moving through the mostly-dark space, the only light inside from the minuscule barred windows. "Witch?" I called, squinting into the darkness.

She wasn't on the bed or in the bathroom area.

"Witch!" I roared, blood starting to pump, wondering if she was like that red-headed one who'd tried to escape, slowly tunneling through the wall. Or like that one with the cat-like eyes who'd hanged herself by her sheets.

I didn't care so much about the witches as a whole, but they'd made an agreement; they'd signed a treaty.

One witch each generation.

To come to us.

They didn't get to run away.

They didn't get to kill themselves.

And it pissed me off when one of them thought they could find a way around the rules.

Anger always started the Change.

As my pulse pounded harder, I could feel my fingers elongating, talons poking out through the tips. My teeth got more pointed, my tongue forked. There was a telltale burning in my shoulder blades, flesh separating, making room for the black wings to start protruding out. The crushing ache in the top of my hairline was the small, blunted horns making their way out of my skull.

The fire burned through me, chasing off the cold that had set in from the endless rain. If you touched my skin, it could nearly burn you.

On a roar, I made my way back to the bed, hand grabbing the bottom, flipping it and flinging it across the room, barely even noticing the sound of the wood cracking and splintering all around.

Then there she was.

Curled in the fetal position on the cold, hard floor, her white dress and cloak wrapping up a tall, but slender body.

The flowers were gone from her hair, and the intricate braids the witches were known for were worked free, leaving her raven hair slightly curled, spilling over her shoulders and back, half concealing her face.

At the roar, or at the sudden disappearance of her hiding place, the witch gasped, jumping up, scrambling away until her back hit the wall, bringing her knees in at her chest, and wrapping her arms protectively around them.

Fuck.

She was a looker.

I didn't remember ever thinking that of any of the others. Maybe because by the time they were let out of the basement, they were older, wilder, their spirits so broken that any beauty they might have possessed seemed dusty and faded.

This woman was fresh.

Dripping with the fruity aroma of youth and the acidic scent of fear.

With the Change on me, I could make out each individual scent. The herb-like smell still clinging to her hair. The salt of sweat. The must of her clothing from being in a cold, enclosed space. And, finally, the fucking intoxicatingly sweet scent of her pussy. Even through the layers of clothes. Even though she wasn't turned on.

Fuck, I couldn't imagine what she would smell like if she was.

Not that I was thinking of fucking a witch.

It went against everything we believed in.

We were on different sides, after all.

Contrary to popular belief, witches weren't the evil ones. These tree-hugging, moon-dancing, earth-loving worshippers of the God and Goddess.

They were the good ones.

Us?

We were the bad guys.

Still.

There was no denying her beauty. It was in the creaminess of her flawless, milk-like skin, in the softly pointed chin, the delicate cupid's-bow mouth with fat, pouty lips, in the delicate nose with the slightly upturned tip, the high cheekbones, the proud forehead, the golden, honey-brown eyes framed by thick black lashes that almost looked fake.

But the witches didn't do fake.

No makeup, no manmade fabrics.

The only thing this witch had that she wasn't born with was that crescent moon tattoo high on her forehead, the tips sneaking up into her hair, small and delicate and a symbol of the life we had taken her away from.

"D-don't r-rape me," the witch stammered, her voice as sweet as the smell of her.

A hiss worked its way out of me, making a shiver course through her.

"Don't be disgusting." To that, those nicely arched brows of hers furrowed. "We don't fuck witches," I informed her, feeling my rage start to dissipate, my body Changing back into the human form that, after all this time, was somehow becoming more comfortable than my true form. Maybe because this environment was not conducive to supporting my true form. That was the only logical explanation.

"A-are you going to e-eat me?"

Well, there was an idea. Though, I was pretty sure the *eating* I had in mind was very different than what she meant. My fucking mouth salivated at my idea, though. My cock was hardening just thinking about it. *That sweet taste on my tongue.*

"If we wouldn't fuck you, why the hell would we eat you?" I shot back, watching the confusion and relief mix together on her face.

"Then what am I doing here?"

"If we don't want to fuck or eat you?" I clarified, snorting. "Because of the treaty."

"Well, yes. But what purpose do I have here?"

"Right now, your purpose is to stop being fucking sad so the goddamn rain will stop."

To that, I was surprised to see a spark of a flame dancing around in those unique eyes of hers.

"I'm supposed to stop being sad," she repeated, voice no longer quivering. If anything, it seemed to be getting stronger.

"Yes."

"When you tore me away from my mother? My family? My friends? My coven? My entire way of life? And then you stuck me in a cold and dingy basement with no way to bathe myself, feeding me animal flesh, and denying me any basic dignity? I'm not supposed to be sad over all of that?"

"Let me rephrase," I said, making my voice firm even if I appreciated the fact that she was all fire and spirit instead of crying and shaking. "I don't give a fuck if you're sad, but make the rain stop."

"I can't control it," she shot back.

"You're a witch. That's what you do."

"Yes, well, I am a very poor witch. That's why I'm here, isn't it? They wouldn't exactly send one of the ones destined for greatness now, would they?"

I'd never given that any thought. Of course they would send us their least talented, their most troublesome. Maybe that was why we'd had issues with so many of them.

"If you can't control it, how will it stop then?" I asked.

"A bath might be a good start."

"A bath."

"I've been down here for a week and haven't been able to get clean. I am starting to smell. It's making me miserable."

She was right about that.

Just wrong about the context.

Maybe humans wouldn't like her smell.

But I was finding it difficult to keep my cock from straining against the fly of my jeans at the heady sweetness emanating from her.

"If I let you go upstairs and bathe, you will stop the rain?"

"It is worth a shot," she suggested, chin lifting up.

"Fine. Fuck it. Let's go."

"Now?"

"Yes, now. Do you have something better to do today? Start a tornado, maybe?" I asked, reaching down to grab her wrist, yanking her up onto her feet, getting a glare for my efforts.

"Maybe I will. Direct it right through this house. Take you and your evil friends out."

"You could try, witch. But not even you can kill us."

"Lenore," she said, grudgingly following behind me as I made my way to the stairs.

"What?"

"My name. It's Lenore. I don't want to be called 'witch' in that way."

That was rich.

"It's cute that you think I give a fuck what you want," I shot back, pushing open the door to the main floor of the house even as I rolled her name around in my head. Lenore. It was pretty. Classic. I liked it more than I had any right to, especially since she was a fucking witch.

"What the hell is this?" Drex asked as we walked past the study where he was reaching once again for the bottle.

We couldn't get drunk.

Not the way humans could.

We could feel a certain sizzle.

But more than that, Drex was attracted to the burn. He said it reminded him of home.

"She thinks a shower might make her less sad," I said, rolling my eyes.

"You said bath," Lenore shot back, stopping in her tracks, folding her arms over her chest.

"Hey, Ly, you have a bath in *your* bedroom, don't you?" Drex asked, smirking, enjoying the hell out of this, apparently.

"Fine, you'll get your bath," I agreed, waving an arm up the stairs, watching as she moved up first. "Tell Minos to stop feeding her 'flesh,'" I told Drex. "Apparently, that makes her sad as well."

"Fucking witches," he said, shaking his head.

"I know," I agreed before following Lenore up the stairs.

"How big is this home?" the witch asked as we walked down the hall on the second floor.

"Don't know. Twelve-thousand square feet. Something like that."

"What could you ever need so much space for?"

"If you don't like the extra space, I'd be happy to toss your ass back in the basement."

She didn't respond to that, save for murmuring under her breath. But I couldn't make out the words.

"This room," I said, waving her into my bedroom. "Through there," I told her, nodding toward the open bathroom door. "No," I called when she went to close the door behind her. "You have to leave the door open." Her eyes blazed at that, her jaw getting tight. "Can't risk you trying to jump out the window, can we? Then we'd have to go back and take one of the other witches. Your mother, maybe," I suggested, enjoying the rage spreading across her face.

Her chin jerked up higher as she stood right there in the doorway, reaching up to undo the tie on her cloak, pushing it back off her shoulders.

I was frozen in the spot as her hands reached down, gathering the skirt of her dress, pulling it upward, baring her slender legs.

My cock stiffened as she kept drawing up the hem, exposing her naked pussy. I guess witches didn't wear underthings. My cock throbbed at that realization even as her hands kept pulling up the dress, showing the soft curve of hip, the slope of her smooth stomach. Then, finally, the swell of her breasts with their pink nipples just begging to be sucked and nipped.

Fuck.

My cock was throbbing for release as she jerked her chin even higher, then turned away, her round ass bouncing as she made her way to the bath, lowering herself down to hide herself before she figured out the faucets.

Witches didn't have running water in the woods.

"Oh!" she said a moment later when, I figured, she found the hot tap.

Then she let out a low, groaning sound as the water started to fill.

I shifted my position so that I could see the mirror over the sink, showing me the reflection of the witch as she leaned backward in the tub, reaching for a bar of soap in a dish that the old housekeeper must have put there.

The witch soaped it up in her hands then ran them down her body, circling over her breasts.

"Fuck," I hissed, reaching down to work my button and zipper free, then inside to free my hard cock, watching the witch bathe herself as I stroked, fantasizing about getting a taste of that sweet-smelling pussy, and feeling her wetness and tight walls around my cock.

I came harder than I think I had in decades.

Maybe ever.

It wasn't until I was done that I realized the witch must have been able to see me in the mirror like I had seen her. She had been watching me jerk-off while she bathed.

She should have been horrified.

But that almost looked like desire in her eyes...

Chapter Three

Lenore

I'd never seen a demon in the flesh.

Sure, there had been the man who brought me my food each day. If I remembered correctly, he'd called himself Minos.

But when he'd come down the stairs, he was in his human flesh.

Minos was striking in appearance. That was the only way I could describe him. He had unusual features that shouldn't have worked together, but somehow did.

He had a square face with deep indents under his cheekbones, a wide mouth, a thin, but proportionate nose, rounded eyes. He had long, dark hair. But the most striking feature of his face was the fact that he had one brown eye and one green. Yet both eyes seemed to have a hint of red in them, which was something I had never seen in humans or witches.

I wondered if it had something to do with being a demon.

But when this new demon came down the stairs, he had shed his human skin, and was partially changed into his demon form.

It should have been terrifying.

And it had been.

The talons, the horns, the strange reddish hint to his skin, the deep, grumbly quality to his voice, the forked tongue.

Terrifying, yes.

That was the point, after all.

To be scary.

But there was something else inside of me when I first laid eyes on him.

It was just as primal as fear.

But unexpected.

Warm instead of cold.

It was a heated sensation across my chest and down my stomach, dipping lower, culminating in a tingling sensation between my thighs.

We were a coven of women. There were no men in our coven. Sometime in our history, maybe during the Burning Times, maybe before, the history was murky, our High Priestesses decided men were a distraction from our purpose, from our powers.

As adults, after we were given our assignments, we were permitted to venture out of the woods to seek the company of men. In a superficial, physical way only.

No feelings.

No love.

Just sex.

Pleasure.

Reproduction, when we decided we were ready.

We only had daughters, continuing the cycle.

And while I had come of age two years before, I had yet to decide I was ready for the touch of a man. Which was likely because my mother, a woman of experience, had sat me down, and informed me that in her history, many of the men she had known the touch of simply didn't know how to touch her body the correct way, to make the primal magic sing across the nerve endings, cause those deep undulations inside.

We had always been empowered about our own pleasure, were taught the ways of our bodies, how we could make them explode with pleasure. Orgasm magic could help difficult rituals, that deep release of energy.

And with her words, followed by the words of some of the girls my age who had ventured out, coming back talking of pain and embarrassment and completion for the man that didn't bring about pleasure for them, I decided to delay that experience for myself, maybe until I thought I was ready to bear my first daughter.

So I wasn't familiar with the connection between desire and the presence of a male figure.

I hadn't been prepared for the heady, intoxicating sensation of it.

I shouldn't have even felt it.

This male was not even a man in the strictest definition.

He was male and he had male parts, but he was not a man.

He was a *demon*.

He was a creature of hell.

He was evil.

He stood against everything my coven and I believed in.

As he stood there as I pulled my clothing off in front of him, I expected to feel humiliation and rage.

What I felt, instead, was a warming sensation, making a flush move across my chest, up my cheeks.

As his hungry gaze moved over my bare body, there was a tightening in my core, making me turn suddenly away, to hide in the tub, focusing a moment to figure out the plumbing that I had heard about, but had never personally experienced.

The coven was, as the regular humans said, *off the grid*.

We had composting toilets, but no running water. Instead, we had wash basins and pitchers. And when we bathed, we either did so in the river, or we filled up a tub we kept near the river, that we then built a fire under.

Running water was one of the few things I was sure, as I lay back and soaped up my body, that the normal people got right.

Just as I was starting to enjoy the sensation of getting clean after feeling unwashed for so many days, a movement in the mirror over the vanity drew my focus. And there at the corner of the mirror, just barely visible, was the demon. Ly, his demon brother had called him. If I recalled my lessons correctly, that made him Lycus. He was second-in-command only to the leader, Ace.

But there he was, looking at the mirror. Looking at *me* in the mirror.

His eyes were intense, his jaw tight, his body rigid. As my gaze moved down the length of his body, I saw the bulge at the fly of his jeans. Even as my focus stayed there, his hand lowered, undid his button and zipper, reached inside, and pulled out his erection.

I might not have had experience with men personally, but I knew just about everything there was to know. We had many anatomically correct male God statues, drawings, and paintings.

In the flesh, as it were, was very different from statues and pictures. Those always made it look hard, yes, but in real life, it looked somehow hard, yet somehow soft at the same time. Like if you ran a hand across it, it would be smooth and warm.

The statues and pictures hadn't prepared me, though, for this.

For this man.

No, this *demon*, I reminded myself.

But regardless of his origins in hell, this flesh he was wearing was all man.

And impressive, at that.

I pressed my thighs together at the length of him, the girth, realizing my hand would barely close around him.

That should have been intimidating, a little worrisome.

But all I felt was a heat, a thrill, a tightening of desire.

As his hand started to stroke his cock, the sensation only grew until it felt like it was overtaking me completely, until there was an oppressive weight on my lower stomach, a throbbing between my thighs that begged for release.

I didn't dare, though, knowing he could see me. It was bad enough I was allowing him to watch, had said nothing about him looking at me while I was nude.

I soaped my hands again, wrinkling my nose a bit at the plain scent of it, so used to the soaps my coven and I made each summer filled with flowers and herbs, earthy and familiar, then ran my hands down my body as Ly kept stroking himself, somehow making his cock get bigger, thicker, as he went.

A jolt moved through me as my hands brushed over my breasts, finding them heavy and sensitive, then drifted lower, over my belly. I raised one leg out of the hot water, soaping it up as I casually watched the mirror, finding Ly's eyes so heavy-lidded they were almost closed in his desire. I washed my other leg. Then my hand moved upward, slipping between my thighs under the guise of completing my washing, but as my fingertips met my cleft, stroked upward to brush over the little bud at the apex of my sex, a wave of pleasure too intense to deny burst from my touch and outward, making my body jolt, making my head loll back, making a surprised whimper escape me.

It was right then, too, that Ly hissed, his lips forming the foreign—yet somehow instinctively sinful-sounding word—*Fuck*—as he reached completion, his body stiffening, his cock producing his seed.

It shouldn't have been thrilling, but that was the sensation that moved through me as I watched.

My gaze stayed on him as he recovered from his release, found a discarded piece of clothing on the floor, and cleaned himself off with it.

Then, I followed his movement as he seemed to be coming into the room.

With me.

A second later, there he was, at the sink, washing his hands as his gaze moved to mine in the mirror.

Nothing about him right then made me think he knew I had been watching him as he had been watching me.

Which meant my reaction should have been shock and outrage for him intruding on a private moment.

"Get out," I demanded, hoping my voice sounded more forceful to him than it did to my own ears.

To that, he switched off the water and turned to face me, pausing for a second, then making his way toward the tub.

"This is my room, witch. That is my tub you are soaking in. You don't make demands here. You don't tell me to do anything, in fact," he warned me, voice steely, cold, even, but I inexplicably felt a heat moving across me at the sound. "This is my water," he went on, squatting down at the side of the tub, running his hand across the surface of the water, making it lap up over my breasts, causing my nipples to harden.

At that, Ly's breath rushed out through his nose, his eyes flashing, seeming redder for a moment as he reached for my hand that was still holding the bar of soap, rested right above the triangle of my sex. He covered my hand and the soap with his, pushing it downward so it slid between my thighs, the touch making my legs shoot out, my back arch, a whimper to escape me.

"That's my soap too," he told me. "Remember that when you're rubbing it across your clit," he added, releasing my hand suddenly, standing, and walking out of the room.

The door to the hallway slammed as well, leaving me wholly alone for the first time since leaving the basement.

My hand released the soap, but stayed between my thighs, my finger teasing over the spot I'd always heard referred to in softer, earthy terms. Bud. Gem. Jewel.

I'd never heard the word he used before.

Clit.

There was something forceful about that word, something primal.

Clit.

I liked it, I decided, as my finger moved across it. I liked it more when he said it in that growling, masculine voice of his, but that was an issue for another time.

Right there, right then, in that tub of water, with my body humming with need, I let my eyes drift closed and brought my body upward in the song of desire, letting it reach the blissful high note that sang through my whole body before I finally finished my bath, washing and rinsing my hair under the running tap. I climbed out of the bath, drying myself off with the scratchy towel on the drying bar before moving over to the vanity, searching around for any creams.

Finding none, I used my finger to brush the chemically minty paste onto my teeth, cleaning them off, washing my hands, slipping into my cloak as a makeshift dress as I washed my gown in the sink, figuring I could hang it to dry in the basement, and that I could rotate the two makeshift outfits anytime they allowed me to bathe.

Unsure what to do next, I made my way out into the bedroom.

I'd never seen the outside of the demons' home, but this room was massive, bigger than my entire home in the woods, dominated by a wooden-framed bed that seemed like four could comfortably sleep on it.

There were wooden dressers, nightstands, and a massive box on the wall I knew of as a television, though I had personally never watched one for more than a few seconds when I'd gone with some of the older women in the coven to town to get some supplies that we couldn't secure any other way.

I moved over toward the windows, drawing back the drapes, seeing the damage of my swirling emotions all around the sprawling grounds—pools of water, broken tree branches, sad-looking rose bushes.

The sun was peeking through the clouds now, though, as the thick blanket of sadness seemed lifted.

I was still uncomfortable, unsure, completely in the dark about what was going to happen to me here.

But if the demon was going to rape me, wouldn't he have done it already? If they were going to murder me, wouldn't that have taken place?

I was starting to wonder if all those scary stories told around a fire were nothing more than tall tales from imaginative minds than actual possibilities.

Though, it might have been too soon to write much of anything off.

These were demons, after all.

Evil through and through.

When Ly didn't return several moments later, I made my way toward the door, pressing my ear to it, trying to hear if anyone was approaching, if he was nearby.

Hearing nothing, I hung up my gown in the bathroom and stood around waiting, figuring there was no way they wanted me walking freely around the home without express permission to do so.

After what seemed like hours passed, my stomach grumbling, my eyelids getting heavy, I slowly lowered myself down on the floor beneath the window, feeling the warmth on my face even as the hardwood cooled my back as I closed my eyes, eventually allowing the previously elusive sleep to claim me.

I dreamed of Samhain—the Summer's end solstice I would be missing this year, along with every other sabbat until the end of my time.

We would honor the dead, the generations of mothers before us. We would set their places at the table while we feasted. Then Marianne would hold a seance, seeing if any of the crossed over wanted to speak to us, guide us.

We would end the night by breaking away for private moments alone under moonlight with our cards in our hands, rolling them out in the Wheel of the Year spread, taking the guidance for the coming year that the universe, the mother, the father, had for us.

It was a happy dream as I saw myself spread in my black gown, my black cloak, my familiar, well-loved cards spread out before me.

It was the message that alarmed me, though.

Because it was a message of love.

We didn't fall in love, witches.

We met men, we grew heavy with daughters from them, and we devoted our lives to our beliefs, taking whatever love was within us, and pouring it into our daughters.

We didn't fall in love.

The cards never spoke to us about it.

But there it was, undeniable.

Ace of Cups, symbolizing new love. Two of cups, repressing learning to open up to another. Queen of Cups, a card speaking of sexuality. The Sun, a happily-ever-after sort of card. The Empress, suggesting children.

All happy.

All pointing toward love.

Until my eyes landed on the final card.

The Devil.

"What the fuck are you doing?" A growling voice startled me from my dream.

My eyes flew open, struggling to focus with the fogginess of sleep still blanketing my mind.

Several things came to me at once.

The sun was down in the windows to my side.

I was freezing because my cloak had fallen open down the middle exposing me completely.

And Ly looked even more intimidating and primal standing over me.

"I... resting," I said, voice thick with sleep.

"On the floor? There's a bed right there," he said, waving toward it.

"You own that bed. And the bedding. And the pillows," I spat, throwing his earlier words at him.

"And I don't own the floor?" he shot back, rolling those entrancing eyes of his. "Being a stubborn ass isn't going to get you far now that you're here," he declared, squatting down, slipping his hands under my body, and lifting me off the floor.

Surprise flooded my system. I hadn't been lifted since I was a little girl. I hadn't been carried since I was a babe. And this, well, this was decidedly different than that.

I felt oddly... small.

And strangely safe.

Which was absurd.

I was in the arms of a demon.

A creature of hell.

Safe was the last thing I was.

But he picked me up. And he carried me as though I weighed nothing more than a dried leaf before stopping at the side of the bed and tossing me onto it.

"Sleep there," he demanded in that grumbly voice of his.

I was starting to miss the basement. The certainty of the days there. Footsteps on the floorboards above, a sink and toilet, halfway edible food on a tray at least once a day, brought down by a man who didn't look for me, didn't notice me, didn't seem interested in harming me in any way.

Here, in this room, on this bed, with this demon prowling around, I had no idea what to expect.

Would he touch me like he'd done in the tub?

Was I in that kind of danger?

If I was, why did the idea send a thrill through me?

Ly moved through his room, grabbing something out of a dresser, then going into the bathroom.

I heard the water turn on, then off a few moments later before he appeared, this time wearing only a pair of loose black cotton pants slung low on his hips, putting the rest of his body on display.

Again, I'd seen pictures and statues. But there was something about the flesh itself that was more appealing. The way his muscles moved under the skin as he walked, the artwork he'd had tattooed into his skin.

"What are you doing?" I heard myself ask as he moved to the other side of the bed.

"Going to sleep," he told me, getting into the bed, rolling onto his back, staring up at the ceiling.

I couldn't think of what to say to that. His temper seemed short-fused. If I asked why he didn't bring me back to the basement, he might get set off.

And if his intentions were simply to go to sleep, there was no harm done there, was there?

This bed was preferable to the one in the basement, especially now that the basement bed was broken. And was more than large enough for both of us to sleep without ever so much as brushing shoulders.

So I rolled onto my side away from him, curled my legs into my chest, and closed my eyes.

But sleep refused to come.

I was too aware of him just a few feet away from me. Despite the space, I could feel the heat of him. It warmed my back in a way that shouldn't have been comforting, since his warmth came from the fiery pits of hell. Yet that was exactly what it was. Comforting. In this cold and drafty house, to feel so much warmth, like falling asleep in front of a winter fire, the heat tingled across your skin, burrowed inside, warmed you to your core.

"Fucking hell," Ly growled some indeterminate time later, making me jump, a little squeak escaping between my lips.

"What?" I asked, pulling the front of my cape closed before I turned to look over at him. There wasn't much light in the room, but his eyes seemed to catch what little there was, glowing redder in the dark.

"How am I supposed to sleep with your stomach growling like that?" he demanded, sounding genuinely angry about it.

"How am I supposed to make it stop growling if I haven't been fed?" I shot back.

My body had never become accustomed to hunger. Our coven participated in fasts for certain rituals, but while others seemed to effortlessly get through the long days of emptiness with ease, I was always tormented by the grumbling of my stomach, the stabbing hunger pangs.

"Fucking witches," he snapped, getting out of bed, moving across the room in the dark, and flicking on the light. "Come on then," he demanded as he opened the door.

I didn't stop to think.

I hopped off the bed and followed behind.

I wasn't going to turn down food if I could get it. Who knew when they would feed me again?

If these demons were willing to show me any sort of kindness, I had to be humble enough to accept it graciously.

It was against their nature, after all.

Chapter Four

Lycus

I wasn't known for my self-control.

That wasn't how we were built.

Self-control wasn't a virtue in our world.

In fact, the utter lack of it was much more desirable.

Why I was showing so much to the fucking witch was beyond me.

I wanted to slip my fingers in her waiting pussy in that tub.

And then I walked back into my room after punishing myself in the gym, to find her passed out on the floor with her fucking cloak open, exposing damn near every desirable part of her body to my hungry gaze.

I wanted to pull out my cock, get down on the floor, yank her legs up onto my thighs, and slam inside her.

Mingled with that desire was something else.

A certain level of, I don't know, concern, for the fact that she was asleep on the cold, hard floor.

I didn't do concern.

I actually didn't even recognize it for what it was at first. Which was why I had yelled at her, had grabbed at her, had tossed her onto the bed.

But as I lay there in the dark, wanting to sleep, my mind was flopping around, going over the reaction to finding her there. Which was when I finally saw my emotions for what they were.

Concern.

Maybe even care?

I cared?

That didn't seem like me, but it was also undeniable.

Because when her stomach started growling, I might have snapped at her again, but what was inside was concern over the last time she had a full meal, that she was uncomfortable, that she wasn't getting the nutrients she needed.

What the fuck was wrong with me?

That was what was rolling through my mind as I led her down the stairs and into the kitchen.

I never spent much time in that room. We didn't need to consume much to stay alive. When we did it, it was usually more for pleasure than necessity.

Which was why the witch's stomach was probably so empty. Yeah, Minos brought her food. But what? And how much? Not enough if her stomach was making that noise.

"Wow." The word rushed out of her before she could stop it as she walked in. She didn't want to be impressed by the home of her captors', but there was also no denying that she was. Most people were.

It was a massive place, once built by some oil tycoon as a third or fourth estate. It was a sprawling stone Tudor-style home sitting on ten acres of mostly-wooded land.

The inside had changed through the decades. Ace was the one of us who stayed up-to-date on human trends, knowing things needed to be right if we were going to do our jobs properly. The humans had to accept us as sone of their own. So our home had to reflect that we were.

At present, the kitchen was a massive, open space. The appliances were stainless steel, the cabinets a cream color, and the countertops everywhere—including on the giant island—were wooden.

To the side was a breakfast area with floor-to-ceiling windows that let you see the river that skirted the tree line that was flanked with ancient Weeping Willows.

"But where is the fire?" she asked, her brows drawing together.

"Mostly, we don't need it," I admitted, but waved her over toward the range, turning the knob, making the gas flames ignite.

"Oh, wow."

"You think that is impressive, you got something to learn about ovens," I informed her, taking a certain sort of pleasure in watching her warm her hands over the flame, her eyes wide with wonder.

We'd been around when the humans first invented indoor stoves. I couldn't remember ever feeling as entranced by their discovery as I felt right now.

Maybe that was simply because it had been so long. All humans, in this country at least, had seen a range before, knew how an oven worked. It was novel to see one who didn't.

I had a strange urge to bring her over to the microwave and the coffee pot and show her how those made life easier as well.

Watching her watch TV for the first time would be interesting as well.

"If you don't, may I?" the witch asked, turning a slightly hopeful gaze toward me.

"May you what?"

"Cook?" she asked, waving toward the flames.

"If you can find something in the fridge to cook, go right ahead."

"The... fridge," she repeated, glancing around, not wanting to ask.

"Refrigerator. They even used to call them ice boxes. Keeps the food cold," I added, pointing toward it.

"Right. Yes. Refrigerator. I know about those," she told me, nodding as she made her way toward it, opening it up.

"What's the problem?"

"This is a lot of flesh," she informed me, her voice sounding pained. Then, under her breath, I could have sworn to whisper to the chicken breasts I knew were in there, "Oh, you poor babies."

Fuck.

What did I get myself into, taking her out of the basement? Now she was going to cry over tomorrow's fucking dinner.

"There is some grass and twigs outside, if you'd prefer."

"I would, actually, prefer grass to flesh," she told me, shooting me a steely-eyed glare. "But there are some root vegetables here that are passable. Do you never tend your garden? Why is nothing fresh?"

"Garden," I scoffed. "Whatever is there comes from the store. Do we look like the gardening sort to you?"

"Do you plan to kill me in the near future?" the witch asked, making me jolt back.

The witches, in my experience, were all about beating-around-the-bush, and pleading, and crying. Never point-blank questions.

"I, ah, we have no immediate plans to kill you," I told her.

"Would I be permitted to start a garden?" she asked. "If you can not or will not supply fresh fruits, vegetables, and grains, I could provide my own, should I have the seeds. Which would be much less expensive for you, as well, than buying fresh foods to keep me alive."

"Money is not an issue. But if tending a garden would keep you from getting sad, I am sure Ace will be fine with it."

"I will be fine with what?" Ace said from behind me, making his way into the kitchen.

"With the witch growing a garden to provide for her meals. So she doesn't continue to get sad and make it rain."

"What an irritating power to possess," he said, shaking his head.

Even though the rain had cleared up, he was still wearing multiple layers—an ancient hand-knitted charcoal sweater over a hooded sweatshirt. He was the oldest of all of us. I wondered if that was why he struggled more with the cold and damp than we did, because he had spent so much more time in hell than any of the rest of us.

"It's quite useful when it is applied appropriately," the witch shot back, getting a raised brow from Ace.

"This one is mouthy," he observed.

"Apparently, they only send us the rejects," I informed him.

"That makes a certain kind of sense, I guess," Ace agreed, moving over toward the coffee machine. Again, we never got a jolt from the caffeine, but like Drex with his liquor, I think Ace liked the warmth. "What?" he snapped, making the witch jolt back from where she had been peering over his shoulder.

"She isn't familiar with appliances," I explained. "And she seems curious in nature."

"That will become irritating," Ace decided, but didn't push her away as he went about making the coffee. "Ever have coffee, witch?" he asked.

"Caffeine is off-limits for us."

"Of course it is," he scoffed. "You truly are an archaic clan."

"We believe in the old ways."

"Only because you haven't experienced the new ones," he shot back.

Ace had always been the most adaptable of all of us. Maybe because he had always been our leader, he felt it was his job to lead us into the future. Until, eventually, we could possibly go back home.

He brought back all the new electronics along with a book to learn to use them, then explained them all to the rest of us who were often not the most captive of audiences.

"Will I be allowed to open a garden?" she asked, ignoring his jab.

To that, Ace sighed, reaching to grab two mugs out of the cabinet.

"If Ly will handle the ordering of supplies as well as babysitting you while you work in said garden, I have no current objections. She should get a kick out of ordering seeds online," he added, shooting me a smirk as he pressed a mug full of hot coffee into the witch's hands before making his way out of the kitchen.

"You can drink it," I told her, moving to grab a cup for myself, switching off the range as I went. "No one here is going to tell on you," I added.

"As if that would stop me," she mumbled into the cup. "It does smell divine." Or at least she thought so until she took a sip and spat it out onto my bare chest. "Oh, oh my. That is... that is awful," she declared, scraping her tongue over the roof of her mouth.

I was not, in general, a man who found humor easily. But I felt a chuckle move up through me at her reaction, as I reached back into a cabinet to produce some sugar—Minos's guilty pleasure—and dropped a couple teaspoons into her cup, giving it a mix. "Try it now," I suggested.

She shot me a distrustful look, but took another sip. "Oh, that is like magic," she declared, giving me a warm smile.

"That is like sugar, actually," I corrected, putting a teaspoon in my mug. "Sugar is natural. How have you ever experienced it?"

"We have honey and fruit sugars," she told me.

"It's not the same."

"No," she agreed, taking another sip. "It is not. But the objection to sugar is the same to alcohol, I believe. They can cause addictions. Addictions make our magic work differently."

"That won't be a concern right now," I told her, leaving off that in a future, when her spirit was broken down a bit, when she was over her objections to being here, her magic would become a big factor.

We'd decided long ago that not telling the witches their fate was the best way to get the results we wanted down the road.

In the past, all that meant was keeping them in the basement, throwing food down to them until they submitted. Which made the whole process all but effortless for us.

This time around, though, there seemed already to be a lot of effort. Bathing and temptation and babysitting and helping the woman pick out fucking garden seeds.

I should have been pissed.

But what I felt, instead, was something akin to eagerness.

It wasn't an unfamiliar emotion. We all felt it leading up to the parties we threw for the MC. When we anticipated finally getting back to our work, our passions, our missions on this earthly plane.

But I rarely felt it outside of those nights.

I stood there watching as the witch moved around the space, chopping up our meager vegetable supply, tssking over our lack of spices, and making the saddest-looking soup I'd ever seen.

"Bring it upstairs," I demanded, already walking in that direction, waiting to make sure she followed behind.

"Eating should be done communally and at a table," she complained as I pointed toward my bed as I went to grab my laptop.

"Tough shit," I said, shrugging. "Here. Seeds," I told her, bringing up the website, turning the screen half toward her.

Her brows furrowed as she looked. "But these are just pictures."

"Yes. And when you hit this button," I said, clicking the 'add to cart,' "those pictures get sent as an order to the person who has the seeds who then packages them up, and sends them here."

"Wouldn't it be easier to save your own seeds?"

"No."

"But—"

"For fuck's sake, just pick the foods you want to grow so I can place the order. It will take a couple days to get here."

I should have known better than to show the internet to someone who had never seen it before. Because an hour later, the cart had over two-hundred dollars worth of seeds collected. I didn't even fucking object when the witch added things like asparagus that took years to grow.

She would be here, after all.

And, I reminded myself, it was all a one-time purchase if she knew how to do shit like save her seeds. She could even build up a seed vault for future witches.

Why the idea of future witches sent a strange, sharp pang through my system was beyond me, though.

"I need to rest if I am going to start the garden tomorrow," the witch declared, taking a deep breath, making her tits press up against the thin material of her cloak, her nipples hardened from the chill in the room. "Are you bringing me back to the basement?"

"No. Just sleep here."

What the fuck?

She *belonged* in the basement.

That was where all the generations of witches went. That was where we'd agreed they belonged. To help the transition, to make sure they became compliant, to break their spirits enough to have them do what needed to be done.

If I allowed her to walk around the estate, make demands, sleeping in my fucking bed, what were the chances that we could break her spirit enough to bend her to our will?

She shifted down in the bed, one of her hands pressed to her full stomach, the other over her head, toying with her hair a bit, the cloak slipping open down to her navel, revealing the outline of her tits. Her eyes drifted closed as she hummed something soothing and ancient—some song of her coven—and I had a startling realization.

I didn't want to break her spirit.

I wanted her to stay just as she was.

What the fuck was that about?

Chapter Five

Lenore

The days stretched long even as the sun moved further away.

On my first full day out of the basement, I opened up a large garden under the watchful eye of Ly. And, as it turned out, I caught most of his demon friends glancing out of windows as I dug up the weedy grass and turned the dirt, sprinkling the grounds of coffee from the kitchen into the soil after asking Ace if it would work like tea did, adding needed elements to the dirt.

It was far too late, of course, to plant a summer garden, but it was early enough in this climate to plant various fall and winter vegetables.

Beets, carrots, onions, broccoli, bush beans, small cucumbers, and salad greens.

Everything else would need to wait until the spring unless I could convince the demons that I could plant some crops in front of the massive windows they had in each of the rooms of their home.

At the very least, some herbs.

I didn't know if the issue was their demonic nature, or simply not knowing how to cook and therefore, what tasted good, but I could not wrap my head around the fact that they did not even have basil or oregano stored for cooking.

Aside from my garden, I wasn't given much to do. There were no elderly to care for, no babies or children to teach, no chores to be carried out.

So on the third day, while Ly was watching something bloody and horrific on that awful television set of his in the living room, I took myself down to the basement, sorting through all the books left there over the years by Ace who, as I learned, was a lover of reading and learning.

True, it made him smug and superior-sounding when you tried to discuss a topic with him, but I was not opposed to learning the ways of this new world I had never known.

I tossed books to the side about governments and economics, choosing instead to read the guides about electronics, about how appliances worked, what the internet was, how the heating worked without fireplaces. I also became fascinated by a thick, old tome with browning pages and patchy ink that talked about The Burning Times and the Inquisition and about how the Old Ways got hidden away. How, over time, humans not only forgot that witches and demons and other creatures existed, but vehemently denied their reality, calling them figments of writers' imaginations, the stuff of children's stories.

No wonder the women of my coven got such strange looks when we went to town, why Marianne had insisted on silence from us if we accompanied her on a trip. Unless we were visiting the stores with the crystals and talismans, incense and candles, where people seemed fascinated by us. Marianne would take a place in a back room and shuffle her cards for waiting women, telling them of their best paths in life, getting money in return, which we used to purchase items we couldn't provide for ourselves. Materials and needles, things of that nature.

But aside from a small niche of women who believed in the cards and gemstones, but not magic in general, everyone else thought witches and our lifestyles were fairy tales.

It was startling to realize the world didn't know you existed. More so, that if they knew you did, they would consider you evil, on par with the demons, not a source of light and good that we truly were.

But I devoured the books Ace had provided. I read until my eyes went blurry, and my head started to hurt, a part of me worried that I would run out of space in my mind to store all this new information.

I was ravenous.

Each day, after working in the garden and bathing, I curled up with a book until I couldn't read anymore.

"Are we sure it's a good idea that the witch learns things?" Drex asked as he walked into the room, going straight to the bottle of whiskey I came to relate to him.

"The witches have always had access to the books," Ace said, looking up from his book.

"Yeah, but none of them used them. Too busy crying or screaming at us."

My heart ached whenever they mentioned the other Sacrifices that came before me. I didn't know them personally, of course. They lived before I was even born. But they had lived here with these demons. And from what I could tell, they were not treated the same way I was being treated. They lived for years in the basement before they were permitted up.

That led me to believe they weren't ever given a chance to bathe fully, had to endure plates full of meat and sad vegetables, they never got to walk outdoors, breathe in fresh air.

I didn't understand why my treatment was so different. Why I had been pulled out of the basement. Why I was allowed to tend a garden, cook my own meals, bathe in Ly's tub.

Things had changed, though.

I didn't understand why, but after three nights of sleeping in Ly's bed, I was banished back to the basement for the evening hours. After the sun went down, and after dinner was made, eaten, and cleaned up after, he snapped at me and led me to the basement, locking me down there.

After being upstairs and allowed to walk mostly free—though Ly's gaze followed me everywhere—it had been easy to forget that I wasn't a guest here. I was a prisoner. I was The Sacrifice. And I still had no idea what that meant to these demons.

I'd heard them speaking of the other Sacrifices. About how long they stayed in the basement. Years, it seemed, before they were permitted upstairs. And, I figured, they were only let up for whatever purpose the demons had for them.

I was the exception, not the rule.

Not so engulfed in my grief now, while I walked around the basement, I was able to see things I missed the last time.

The hanging flowers, even some herbs that must have been found wild in the woods. The love and care that was put into the alter. There were murals on the walls. The pentacle. A wheel of the year.

Then, nearly hidden behind an old cloak was a list.

Names.

The names of many of the Sacrifices before me as well as little details about them. Favorite seasons. Favorite colors. Favorite tarot cards.

Curious, I moved around the mostly-empty space, foraging for any other possible traces of the women before me, clues as to what happened to them, what their sacrifice ended up being.

I'd gotten the nerve up to ask Ly once what the plan was for me.

He'd gruffly informed me that I would "know when I needed to know, so don't ask again."

I'd been at the house for almost two weeks at that point, and while I hadn't seen any true evil behavior from the demons—no women were raped, no men were tortured, no satanic rituals were performed—I had found them, as a whole, to be cocky, condescending, and rude. Not damnable offenses, but frustrating when you lived with them.

I was actually feeling a bit of guilt for often being too outspoken, too impatient, too disruptive. To my mom, to my coven. I should have been a better daughter, a better community member. I should have been quieter, calmer, more patient.

Had I been, I would still be at home.

At this time of day, I would have been in the garden, raking up potatoes, pulling up carrots, carefully storing them in packed dirt in the root cellars for the winter.

That said, if I had been a good member of my coven, someone else would be here in this place. And maybe she wouldn't have been strong enough to ask for a proper bath, or to ask to open a garden to provide food for herself. Maybe she wouldn't have been provided the freedoms to walk around up in the main house.

Because, from what I could see gathered around in the basement, it seemed like most—if not all—of the Sacrifices before me had been tossed in this basement to rot for some untold amount of time.

Until, one day, they were gone from here.

And I couldn't help but wonder how and why.

Where did they go?

What had been done to them?

Surely, the demons wouldn't take a Sacrifice each generation only to throw them in a basement to die of old age.

That didn't seem in-line with what demons were known for.

Evil.

Then again, what was more evil than taking a witch away from her coven, from her community, and her family, and sticking her down in a basement to feel her life slipping away day after day, week after week, year after year?

Maybe they fed off the misery.

Why, then, did Ly bring me out of the basement when my misery was blanketing the world in rain? Shouldn't they have been reveling in that grief?

None of it made any sense.

As much as I could tell, none of the witches had left behind accounts of their lives. There were no instruments to write with down here, and if they weren't given the freedom to roam, there would have been no way to find something to write with.

The murals on the walls had been made with berries of some sort, precious bits of food they could have eaten to sustain their bodies in the cold, damp space. But they used them to create some beauty in their dark world, to honor the world they came from.

My heart ached for them as I kneeled down in front of the altar, running my hand over the items carefully gathered there.

"Fucking *what* now?" Ly's voice growled as he charged down the stairs, his heavy boots clomping down the steps.

"What?" I asked, startled. My hand went to my hammering heart as I took a steadying breath.
"Ace is going to lose his shit if the rain keeps going."
"Oh," I said glancing over toward the window, seeing the fat raindrops already falling.
"We have company tonight. We can't have it fucking pouring again. It would ruin the mood."
"I... I can't just turn it off," I told him. I never could. When my cat passed away when I was a girl, I wept for a week straight, causing floods that washed out part of our winter food storage. Nothing anyone did could stop it. "I have never had great control over my powers," I admitted.
"Or your emotions. Fucking witches," Ly growled, raking a hand through his hair. "Do you need a bath?" he asked.
"Baths aren't the magical cure to bad moods, you know," I informed him. "Back in my coven, they were simply a part of daily life."
"It worked last time."
"That was different. I felt different. I was sad for different reasons."
To that, I got a sigh before he reached out, grabbing my arm, pulling me up the stairs.
"Lycus!" Ace roared from his usual position in his library.
"I'm working on it," Ly called back.
"Work faster. We were supposed to open the pool and hot tub for the party."
"What kind of party?" I asked as Ly pulled me into the kitchen.
"A party party."
"For what occasion?"

"No occasion."

"You are not celebrating anything?"

"No. We are having people over to eat and drink and dance and flirt and fight and fuck. You know... party."

"Can I come?"

"To the party?" he asked, eyes squinting.

"Yes, to the party. Having something to look forward to may help my bad mood."

I was being manipulative. I remember Marianne throwing that word at me a lot as a teenager when I managed to convince the girls my age to do chores I didn't like for me or join in on my little acts of rebellion.

I had always been good at convincing people to do things I wanted, even when I knew it was not the kind thing to do.

It was yet another reason I was here with the demons.

But it was also a way for me to make a bad situation a bit more tolerable.

Making demands had gotten me out of the basement for some part of the day. It got me the garden. It allowed me to prepare my own foods.

I had no idea what may lie ahead for me, but at least until then, I could enjoy a halfway tolerable existence.

"Ace won't like it."

"Does Ace have to know?" I asked.

"It's not like you blend in with normal human beings."

"I won't speak to anyone."

"That would be a welcome change," he grumbled. "This," he went on, waving toward my body, clad in my white gown.

"If I had something else to wear, I would."

"I will think about it. Is that good enough?" he asked, looking out the window. "Fuck. Guess not," he hissed, shaking his head. "Fine. Fucking fine. You can come. I will have to go and find you something to wear. You will need to keep your head down, stay away from everyone. Just watch."

"Okay," I agreed, excitement starting to bubble up in my system, making the rain slow up, the sun already peeking through the clouds.

"Do I want to know what you had to promise her to make it stop?" Ace asked, coming into the kitchen, moving right to the coffee pot, constantly needing the warmth the beverage provided.

"No."

"Then I won't ask," Ace said, shaking his head. "She doesn't leave the grounds."

"I know," Ly agreed, leading me out of the kitchen, pulling me with him up the stairs and into his bedroom. "Bathe," he demanded, waving toward the bathroom. "I will figure out the other shit."

I had no idea what the "other shit" was, but I was happy to run a bath while he left, slipping into the water, feeling the ache from the bed on the floor in the basement easing away with each passing moment.

I drained the water and refilled it once before washing my hair and climbing out, slipping under the soft covers while the house seemed to come alive around and below me.

Typically, I found the demons rather slothful, always hanging around, drinking, reading, or watching television. I heard the soft strum of a string instrument—knowing these demons, likely a guitar—from somewhere behind a closed door on occasion, but they never did any cleaning, cooking, or yard work.

I was starting to believe they weren't capable.

But from my position on the bed, I could see Ace and Drex moving around the back of the grounds, scooping leaves out of the pool, and placing tables and chairs around.

From below, I could hear the shuffling of furniture, music thrumming then stopping, then starting again, but louder, the beat pulsing up the walls, making even the bed vibrate with it.

It was a long while later when I heard a strange rustling noise along with footsteps on the floors outside Ly's bedroom for a second before it opened and Ly moved inside.

The bags in his hands were what was making the rustling noise, half a dozen of them.

"What is all this?" I asked as he made his way to the foot of the bed, dropping all the bags there.

"Things to wear."

"I can't imagine I will need all of that for one night."

"No," he agreed. "But you will need other things soon. Boots, for the gardening. A jacket for the same reason. You would be useless to us if you caught a chill and died."

The gestures had started out kind, at least. And I was too pleased at the idea of something new to wear to care about his comments.

"There are also things for the bath. Some food. Makeup shit."

"Makeup," I repeated.

"The shit chicks put on their faces. Makes their eyes bigger and their lips redder."

"Oh, right," I agreed, feeling foolish.

We didn't have makeup, not in the strictest definition of the word, but we did use natural dyes on our faces for special occasions, even though we had no one to impress but ourselves.

"You'll figure it out," he said, reading the confusion on my face. "Or make yourself look like a clown. Either way, it will keep you out of our hair while we set things up."

"How will I know when to come down?"

"When I come to get you."

"How long?"

"However long it takes, witch," he snapped, walking to the door, leaving, slamming it on his way back.

He always blew hot and cold with me.

On the one hand, he had gone out, spent his money, and bought me more things than I needed, including an abundance of fresh fruits and vegetables as well as some bottled fruit drinks. *Smoothies*, they said.

I knew very well that he didn't need to buy me these things. The other witches did not seem to have the same treatment I had been enjoying.

So he didn't have to be kind.

But he was.

And, I was starting to suspect, anytime he caught himself being kind, he covered it by being especially gruff.

It couldn't have come naturally to him—a creature of pure evil—to be considerate, to think of others ahead of himself.

Even if his reasons were, at their core, selfish, since they didn't want rain, so that their party could be enjoyable. Which, I imagined, served their own pride in some way.

Still, it was nice.

And I was going to let myself feel appreciative. If for no other reason than it *felt* good to feel appreciation for a kind gesture.

I grabbed the bag of sugar snap peas and made my way into the bathroom with all the packages, looking over the makeup items, trying to discern what might be used for what, then snacking while I worked on my face, seeing a new me emerge as I went.

My eyes looked bigger with the liner, my lashes thicker and darker with the mascara, my lips a red that reminded me of flowers, a dramatic change that had my lips seeming a more prominent feature.

I liked the woman looking back at me. She looked more worldly and confident.

The only remnants of the witch in the woods seemed to be the blue of my half-moon tattoo and my long, dark hair.

Finished, I moved onto the clothing selections, finding myself perhaps more baffled than I had been about the makeup which, at least, explained itself on the packaging.

Clothing had always been simple in my coven. We wore gowns—lightweight linen in the summer and heavy wool in the winter—and cloaks. If we were especially cold in the winter, we had stockings to slip under our gowns.

We didn't wear undergarments save for when our sacred moontime arrived, making us use thick pads of fabric between our legs.

So this strange collection of clothing had me using basic reasoning skills to figure out.

The piece that baffled me most was two circular bits of lacy fabric with a black lining, two straps, and a band around the bottom.

Eventually, though, I figured it—and its troubling clasps—out, finding it supportive, if a bit restrictive.

A breast covering.

For modesty, I imagined.

That was something that had never been an issue in the coven. With no men around, there was nothing to feel modest about. We all had the same parts, more or less. And we faced nothing to fear from showing those parts of ourselves.

But in this world, where men and women mingled, I imagined modesty was necessary to avoid the unwanted attention of the base of menfolk, the type we were warned about with grave voices, our elders telling us the ways in which a man's body could hurt a woman, how some human men were hardly better than wild beasts.

Regardless of the restriction—and the unpleasant cultural associations with regard to it— I liked the garment. It showed off my stomach, the flare of my hip.

It felt daring, sexy.

Going back to the clothing, I found what, by process of elimination, I figured was a skirt. Even if I had never seen one so short or made of such material before. It was black, thin, stiff, and strangely shiny. When I slipped it up my legs, it only managed to fall about halfway down my thigh.

Digging through the remaining bags, I found sprays that smelled chemical and flowery at the same time. Choosing the one the smelled the most like an actual flower—lavender—I sprayed some on my mostly-bare chest before going back into the bags to find some strange foaming product in a can and a razor. A razor, at least, I was familiar with. We used them to shave the heads of the sisters who aimed to become more devoted to the gods, the women who lived fully in the woods, without shelter, without having their daughters, their entire lives dedicated to the land, to their studies of it, and to their spirituality.

And I knew from one of Ace's books about 'feminism' that women in this modern world had started to shave off nearly all of their body hair.

Looking at myself in the large mirror, I could see the hair on my legs that had been allowed to grow as it did naturally my whole life. The same was true under my arms. Between my legs.

Not wanting to be seen as backward, not wanting to stand out, I slipped back out of my skirt, went into the shower to get wet as the directions demanded, and put the foaming product up and down my legs, under my arms, and between my thighs. Then I working the razor blade across my skin.

When I was done, there was blood everywhere. On my skin. In the shower. On the floor as I walked back out, slipping back into the skirt as I tried to think of a way to stop the bleeding when I didn't have any of my usual remedies around.

"What the fuck are you wearing?" Ly asked, voice a strange, low hiss, sounding oddly airless.

"The clothes you brought me," I supplied, waving an arm toward the bags. "Will I not fit in?" I asked, brows furrowing.

"Fuck," he said, sighing, raking a hand through his hair. "You will," he told me.

"Then what's wrong?"

"Here. Just... you need this," he told me, brushing past me to go toward the bags when, suddenly, his nose scrunched up as he sniffed the air, his gaze shooting down to the floor. "Are you bleeding?" he asked. "Did you hurt yourself?" he demanded, grabbing my arm, and yanking me around.

"Oh, I, uhm... I tried the razor," I admitted, feeling the heat rise up my neck, blooming across my cheeks. "It was my first time," I added as his gaze slid to my legs, seeing the blood.

"Christ. You cut yourself more than you didn't," he grumbled, dropping down to a crouch, calloused palm grabbing the back of my calf so he could inspect my cuts.

"What?" I asked, stiffening when he angled his head up, taking another deep breath, his nostrils flaring, his eyes blazing redder.

"Panties," he rumbled.

"I don't understand."

I would swear he said, "Of course not," but his voice was too quiet as the hand on my calf lifted, and pulled outward, spreading my thigh wide as his body arched upward.

And his face... his face went between my legs.

Not a second later, I could feel the most delicious, scandalous friction, something smooth and intimate, sliding up the cleft of my sex, teasing at the apex for the barest of seconds, the suddenly forked ends circling that bud of desire.

My thighs started to shake.

But it was over before I could truly wrap my head around what was happening.

His tongue was on the most intimate part of me.

But then it wasn't, and he was looking up at me.

"Panties would prevent me from doing that," he told me as he put my leg back down.

As he got to his feet and turned his back on me, I couldn't stop one thought from crossing my mind.

Why would I want to prevent him from doing that?

Except, of course, that he was evil.

And he might very well torture or kill me in the future.

"Put this on over the bra," Ly demanded, tossing a deep mauve velvet jacket at me.

Trying to shake the lingering desire clawing at me, I slipped on the jacket, finding there was no way to clasp the front, creating a peek-a-boo effect.

"Better?" I asked, turning to find him standing in the doorway. Almost, maybe, as though he didn't trust himself to be close to me.

In response, I got a grunting noise.

"Will I fit in?" I asked.

"Enough. But you have to follow the rules. No talking to anyone. And stay away from Ace."

"I can do that. Am I allowed outside? To see the pool? And the outdoor tub?"

"Hot tub," he corrected. "Only if I am there to watch you. Otherwise, you stay inside. Hug the walls."

"How does one hug a wall?"

"It means stay near the walls. Don't get involved in anything."

"Okay. When may I come down?"

"Later," he said, nodding at me then turning, and walking away.

All thoughts of the cuts on my legs vanished.

Anticipation skittered across my nerves.

I had no idea what was in store for me that evening.

Had I known, I wouldn't have left the room.

Chapter Six

Lycus

The parties were important.

The parties were work, under the guise of reckless fun.

We'd been walking this shithole of a human plane for generations. The first couple of those we did so simply creating chaos where we could. But as the humans progressed, it became harder to get away with the things we did. And as pesky as human law enforcement was, things got complicated when we were thrown behind bars and didn't rot like they wanted us to.

So we got smarter about it.

Eventually, came the emergence of motorcycle clubs, and the debauchery bikers were known for.

They liked to fight and fuck and drink and snort and shoot and all the things we loved it when humans did.

And the best part?

Others outside of the lifestyle found themselves inexplicably drawn to these men and their rough—and often lawless—ways.

That was where the fun came in.

That was where *we* came in.

So, we bought bikes.

We had cuts made.

We went to the rallies and rubbed shoulders with other MCs.

And, when the mystery was strong enough, we would throw a massive party.

They were the nights of the year when we felt near fully ourselves again.

"When are Aram and Red coming back?" Drex asked, lounging in his usual jeans and tee, but with his leather cut over it this time, his one-percent badge on his chest.

"Seven said they were on their way," Ace supplied, dressed more down than usual to match the aesthetic needed for the evening, looking more like Drex, and already miserable without added layers to keep warm. Knowing him, he would spend a good portion of the night in the hot tub, screwing hot, naked women, whispering things in their ears, bringing ideas to their heads they never would have thought on their own.

And that was the plan.

To bring out the buried—or sometimes not so buried—innate evil in humans. They all had it. Their selfishness, their pride, their bitterness, their hatred.

It was surprisingly easy to bring those parts of them to the surface, to toy with them, to stoke the flames of them until they burned bright.

Until there was no goodness left.

Until they were wicked through and through.

They would live out the rest of their lives sinning. And at the end, when their souls left their bodies, they would go to hell.

It was the closest we could all get to revisiting.

It was a way to stay connected to who we truly are, despite being so long stuck on this earthly plane.

Some day, when the veil between worlds opened up again for us, we would go back home as heroes, thousands of wicked souls to our names.

Plus, it was some fucking fun for a change.

Normally, we were all in fantastic moods on the hours leading up to a party.

And, to be fair, the others were.

Well, Ace, Drex, and Seven were.

Minos, as usual, was still in his room, keeping to himself. The longer we were on this human plane, the less often any of us saw him.

He would come out for the party, of course. He would do his part. He might even find some joy in it, even though you would never know it.

I would usually be excited to find new ways to corrupt those who were already so heavily leaning toward evil rather than good.

But, I found myself excited for another reason.

An unexpected and unacceptable reason.

That reason was one floor ahead wearing a bra, miniskirt, and a velvet jacket, covered in shaving cuts and looking even more tempting than usual with her makeup applied, and her hair left long instead of in braids.

I was regretting agreeing to allow her to come to the party.

She would be noticed.

Even with my demands that she stay silent and hug the walls, I knew that people would see her. She would stand out. There was something unique about her, something that drew you in.

It drew me in.

It kept fucking drawing me in.

It made no sense.

Yes, she was beautiful.

But I had known many, many beautiful women in my time. And I had never felt the pull I felt toward this fucking witch.

God, that scent of hers.

Sweet like ripe fruit.

I hadn't been able to hold myself back from getting one small taste of her.

She exploded across my tastebuds, instantly intoxicating. And it wasn't possible for me to feel that way.

Yet, I did.

One taste of her.

And I felt addicted.

Each moment was like going through withdrawal.

What was that?

Was it her magic?

No.

That made no sense.

I'd known all the other witches. They had never affected me this way. Not even when they were using their magic.

Their magic didn't smell sweet.

It smelt smoky, almost, like wood burning.

It wasn't something I felt drawn to. If anything, it was overpowering, a little off-putting.

So this scent, it was all her own. And that was somehow even more problematic.

"Fuck," I hissed, getting up to get a drink.

"What's with you?" Drex asked as I stole his bottle.

"I don't know," I admitted. "But—" I started, before hearing the grumble of the bikes as they came down the road.

"Here comes trouble," Ace said, taking a deep breath like a stressed-out father when he was preparing for his kids to cause problems.

And, to be fair, Red and Aram were the youngest and wildest of all of us. They had barely had a chance to really enjoy hell before we were stuck on this human plane.

So they were having fun raising hell on earth while we were homesick.

The bike engines cut off, and the front doors burst open to the sound of Red's throaty laughter.

"Anybody home?" she called a second before sauntering into the study. "So predictable," she said, sighing.

Red was almost absurdly good-looking. It made her good at what she did in this club. She was tall and lean with big tits, nice hips, and a round ass. Her face was an inverted triangle, a wide forehead with a softly pointed jaw. She had high cheekbones under bright blue eyes. And her hair was an almost unnatural shade of red, the flicker of flames in a fire, which she wore long and curly down near to her waist.

Aram was darker-skinned, black-haired, black-eyed, tall, fit, and covered in tattoos that he would only have to have re-stuck in a couple decades, but I guess the bastard just liked the look. And the pain.

But, like Drex, Aram was always up for a fight, got off on the bloodshed, and the ache after. No matter how short lived.

"Did we miss anything?" Red asked, reaching for a bottle of vodka, and throwing some back.

"The new witch is here," Ace said.

"Does this one cry all night?" Red asked, lip curling.

"She makes it pour rain when she's sad," Ace told them, sighing.

"Drag," Red said, rolling her eyes. "Glad she's not in a shit mood tonight. Aram and I have been working overtime to get people to come tonight. It should be packed."

"Good," Drex said, standing, cracking his neck. "I'm itching to do a little corrupting," he said, winking at Red.

"Who set up the music?" Aram asked, casting a dubious glance around the room. "Don't say it is Minos. That angsty shit nearly ruined the last party."

"Ace did," I supplied.

"Shit," Aram complained, sighing, running a hand through his hair. "It's not all classical is it? I am going to look it over," he said before Ace could respond, moving off to do so.

"Speaking of Minos, where is our resident curmudgeon?" Red asked, looking around.

"You know him," Ace said, shrugging. "He doesn't come out until the guests arrive."

"Alright. Well, I am going to go slip into something to make all the seats wet," Red said, smirking at us before sashaying out of the room.

"The kids are home," Ace said, sighing.

"They do half the work for us," I said, shrugging. "Remember when we all had to go to the rallies nonstop?"

"Don't remind me," Ace said, grimacing.

He made a terrible biker. He was a little too well-spoken, a little too into his books. He'd never fit in with the outwardly rough-and-tumble biker sort.

That said, the human bikers would shit themselves if they knew the real Ace, and if they knew the evil, twisted shit he liked to do. If we ever got back to hell, countless of those bastards would see first-hand what frauds they were, and how legit he was.

"Sounds like they're arriving," Drex said, nodding toward the driveway where a couple people were rolling up on bikes.

Anticipation sizzled across my skin as the house started to fill up, as liquor started to pour, and music pounded.

Within an hour of the first person arriving, the place was packed. Women gyrated, skinny-dipped, flashed their tits to anyone who asked.

Men fought, drank, and watched the women.

As for us?

Well, we did what we did best.

We brought out their wicked.

We whispered in their ears, we supplied their drinks and drugs.

It wasn't until nearly two hours into the party that I remembered the witch upstairs.

"Shit," I hissed, looking up at the sky, hoping she wasn't already getting all fucking weepy. I rushed up the stairs, opening the door, and finding her standing facing the windows, munching on some fucking apple slices.

"Can I come down now?" she asked.

"Yeah. But remember the rules. No talking. Stay unseen."

"You have a lot of friends," she said as we made our way down the stairs.

"I don't know any of them. This is a night for work. Alright. Go," I demanded, waving a hand out, seeing Minos coming around the corner, not wanting him to see me with the witch, to draw conclusions.

"You're kinda hot," a warm voice whispered in my ear as I watched two bikers staring off at each other over a game of cards. They just needed the smallest of urges to come to blows, to start a war between their MCs. It would be short and easy work.

"Yeah?" I asked, turning to her, finding what I expected. The women here were always the same. Pretty in a forgettable way, their tits on full display, jeans so tight you could see their fucking pussies through them.

All these years on the earthly plane, one thing that didn't really get old was sex.

All it usually took was a smile like this chick was giving me, one full of scandalous promise, to get me hard and aching for it.

Any other party, I would have pushed her onto her knees in front of me, pulled out my cock, and let her suck me off right then and there.

No one would even notice. People fucked in every corner of these parties.

But even with her looking at me with those promising eyes, I felt nothing. Not a stirring. Jack shit.

What the fuck was going on?

Even as I thought it, a figure came into view, walking with her back plastered to the wall, eyes huge, lips parted at whatever she was looking at. I couldn't see it myself with the wall blocking my view, but I couldn't help but wonder what she was looking at. At one of these parties, anything was possible.

"What do you think of him?" I asked, turning the girl, pointing toward Minos.

"Ohhh," she said, the sound vibrating through her.

What can I say?

Minos might not have had much going for him in the personality department, but he was always the best looking fucker in a room.

He towered over the rest of us, all long dark hair and corded muscles.

And in this generation, the women dug his beard, the fact that he would braid his hair, wear it up, that they could run their fingers through it.

"Yeah. Go get 'im," I suggested, already turning, making my way toward the witch.

I was a solid ten feet away when I could smell her.

Fucking pineapples and watermelon and ripe peaches, that was what she smelled like right then. Sweet and dripping down the chin.

I was hard from two yards away.

She turned slightly, following whatever she was watching, allowing me to move in behind her, look over her shoulder.

And there they were.

A man and a woman the next room over.

She had her tits out the top of her tube top, her skirt yanked up around her waist, getting plowed from behind by some random guy whose name I doubt she knew.

That made sense, didn't it?

She was turned on.

That was why her scent was stronger.

She was turned on watching these other people fuck.

How overpowering would her scent be if, instead of touching, instead of just getting a taste, I made her come?

I guess I would just have to find out, wouldn't I?

Chapter Seven

Lenore

It was difficult to think.

I wasn't sure how people enjoyed having their music so loud that it made your ears hurt.

I figured, after walking around the house for a while, that perhaps they liked the music so loud because they didn't want to actually speak to one another.

I saw and heard very little conversation.

These people appeared to be communicating nonverbally.

Apparently, all the women needed to do was look at a man, giving him a small smile, and he knew that meant he was allowed to approach. And approach they did. Time after time after time. Even when they got rejected more than a few times.

I guess it was a game of odds, finding a mate. If you approached enough of them, surely one would want you.

Watching the men and women interact was my favorite part of the evening.

I didn't like how the men interacted with one another. It was brutish and reminiscent of how cocks would fight if our flock of hens was too small, always looking for a reason to scuffle, or simply having no reason at all other than wanting to prove themselves as the bigger and meaner of their kind.

It was base and off-putting to watch that behavior in human beings. So whenever I entered a room where that seemed to be the main event, I moved onto the next room.

The women with other women in this world seemed little better than the men with men.

Sure, there seemed to be friend groups, but the basis of them appeared shallow and easily shaken. If both women found themselves attracted to the same man, it looked like that was reason enough for them to be angry with each other.

Who wanted friendship that shallow? Especially when there was no shortage of attractive men around.

I wouldn't have thought I was any judge of such a thing, never having been exposed to many men in my life.

Apparently, though, it was something innate, encoded in me. I instinctively knew which men were attractive by the skittering sensation of my heart.

But, by my estimates, there were far more attractive men than unattractive ones, so I couldn't imagine why the attention of one of them was so important as to impact a friendship.

Perhaps in this world, though, men were more important than friendships.

My heart ached at the very idea.

Which was why I turned away from the spaces where those were the things I noticed most.

Which left me with the men and women.

And how they interacted.

Sometimes, it seemed like a sort of dance, a back and forth, a give and take.

Other times, though, it appeared immediate.

A man would approach a woman and after maybe only a couple of moments, they were locked in a kiss, hungry hands roaming over bodies.

No one had ever informed me that this was how men and women interacted, that they pawed at each other in public places. In the stories I had been told, intimacy was something for behind closed doors, between a man and a woman, with no one around to witness what they shared.

It sounded sweet.

This, though?

There was nothing sweet about these couples.

They seemed hot and hungry and unable to control their reactions to each other.

I saw hands going up shirts, down pants.

I saw a woman get pushed to her knees as a man exposed himself to her. And then she closed her mouth around him, moved her lips up and down him until the man's body tensed, and he hissed something out.

It was shocking, to say the least.

I never could have imagined that women did that to men.

Then again, Lycus had run his tongue up my sex only hours before, so I guess I shouldn't have been so surprised.

After that couple, I moved to another room, finding a different couple. The man already had the woman's top down, had his lips sucking on her breasts the way a babe might, while the woman whimpered and begged him to "fuck" her.

Then, his hands were yanking up her skirt, pulling down her "panties," as Ly had called them, then pulling out his hard length, turning her, then slamming inside.

I could feel my own muscles tense in response, a primal urge for fullness, a need that felt nearly undeniable.

"Enjoying the party?" a deep, familiar voice asked from directly behind me, breath warm on my ear, sending a jolt through my system. Surprise, sure, but I had a feeling there was something else as well. Anticipation? Maybe a little guilt at being caught watching the couple, even if they were doing nothing to keep their actions private.

"I, ah," I started, unsure what to say.

"It's okay to watch," he told me, moving in closer, his whole front against my back. "They would get a room if they wanted privacy," he added, taking a deep breath, letting out a low, growling sound, something that made the ache between my thighs even stronger.

"Do people do this in public often?" I asked, and maybe while I did so, I leaned back. But just a little.

"Normally? No. At these parties? Yes," he told me, arm going around my waist as the woman moaned louder, slamming her hips backward as the man thrust inside. "You like watching."

"I didn't say that."

"You didn't need to. I can smell how turned on you are. How much do you want to bet that if my hand drifted down," he said, his fingers teasing over my lower stomach, "I would find your pussy drenched?"

My chest felt tight, my breath coming out too hard, too fast.

I could feel myself relaxing against him, my body inviting more closeness, as my head rested on his strong shoulder.

He took the movement as permission, his hand slipping under my skirt.

"I thought I told you to put on panties," he said as his finger traced my slick cleft. "Or were you just waiting for me to do this?" he asked, his thumb moving over my clit.

I couldn't seem to find the words—or the desire—to tell him to move his hand, to stop taking liberties, or to leave me alone.

Because as his finger started teasing little circles around me, all there was in the world was that sensation, that exquisite building, the promise of something worth the wait in the end.

My head turned on his chest, face nuzzling into his neck, breathing in the fiery scent of him as his free arm rose, slid across my belly, then up and into my bra, squeezing my breast with pressure that was just shy of painful, sending another jolt of desire through my system.

My eyes drifted close, allowing me to melt away into the sensations, to blank out everything else that, suddenly, no longer mattered.

Ly's thumb and forefinger squeezed the tightened bud of my nipple before starting to roll it as one of his fingers started to drift down my cleft, tapping against the entrance to my body.

"Tell me you want my finger to fuck you, *witch*," he demanded, voice in my ear.

He used the word like he always did, like an insult, like a slur. It shouldn't have, but somehow, in that moment, it only made the fire burn hotter through my system.

"Yes," I hissed, my hips starting to rock against his hand, needing more.

"No. You need to say it," he demanded, teasing the tip of his finger inside of me before retreating. "Tell me you want me to finger fuck your pussy," he told me as his thumb pressed a little harder against my clit.

His words were base and filthy.

But there was no denying their truth.

Squeezing my eyes closed a little tighter, I took a steadying breath. "I want you to finger fuck my pussy," I repeated, feeling my cheeks heat in embarrassment.

"That's a good witch," he told me, finger thrusting inside me.

All thoughts of embarrassment evaporated at the sensation, at the unfamiliar fullness inside, the rough but somehow gentle invasion.

A low, rumbling growl worked its way through Lycus's chest and into my body as his finger settled inside, doing a small little turn once seated.

"Fuck," he hissed, his body going tight as his hips shifted, grinding his hard length against my backside, the proof of his desire even more fuel for the fire. "You're so tight," he added, making those muscles inside clench around him. "Can't imagine how good my cock would feel. Here," he added, flicking his finger. "Like this," he went on, withdrawing his finger then thrusting it back in.

His finger was relentless then, nearly slipping all the way out before going back in, fast and consistent, driving my body upward, making my breath get caught, my legs feel weak.

"You want another finger, don't you?"

I didn't know what I needed. Other than release from the torment building inside.

"Y-yes," I whimpered, my hips grinding down on his hand.

Another finger slipped downward as his other finger pulled out. When he thrust back in, there was even more fullness, a slight pinch accompanying it that evaporated almost instantly as the new sensation built, stronger and stronger as his thumb continued to work circles over my clit.

"You want to come, don't you?"

Come.

That sounded like the right word for what I wanted to do.

"Yes," I gasped, one of my hands grabbing the wrist of the one up my skirt, the other lifting, wrapping around the back of his neck, holding on as my leg muscles started to shake.

"Thought so," he agreed, his fingers twisting inside of me. "Your walls are so fucking tight," he added as his fingers crooked inside me, raking against my top wall, causing a new, unexpected sensation. "Yeah," he said when I cried out—a pleased but confused sound. "That's your G-spot," he told me as his fingers raked across it again. "Feels good, yeah?" he asked, his voice rough.

"Yes," I cried out, shameless in my need for release.

"Come," he demanded, his voice a deep, strangled sound, as his fingers continued their sweet torment. "Come, Lenore," he demanded, my name velvet on his lips.

And just like that, I did.

And I did with what seemed like my whole body.

The pleasure started at the base of my spine and spread outward until it overtook me completely, stealing the strength from my legs as the waves crashed through me.

I was vaguely aware of crying out his name at the apex of the orgasm, my fingers clawing at him, holding on for dear life as it felt like I shattered apart.

"Alright," Ly said, voice almost... coaxing—even if that didn't seem like something he was capable of—as I came back down into my body, gasping for air, body trembling wildly, seemingly out of my control. "You're alright," he added, his arm anchoring more tightly around my midsection as his fingers slid out of me, out of my skirt.

"I'm shaking," I told him, as though he couldn't feel that for himself.

"Aftershocks," he told me, and I could feel him shrugging it off.

Aftershocks.

That was an apt way of describing how I felt.

Shaken *after*.

"It'll stop," he added as they continued, and as I continued to cling, not trusting my legs to hold my weight.

"Who are you corrupting now?" a female voice asked, making Ly instantly tense. Which, in turn, made me do the same, my stomach wobbling as Ly let out a quiet, "Fuck."

"Red, fuck off," he demanded, turning slightly, seeming to try to hide me.

It was right then that I remembered where we were, that there were other people around, and I had a role to play.

"Why should you get to have all the fun? I want to talk to her too."

"No," Lycus said, turning me to face his chest completely, his arm roping around my lower back as his other hand grabbed the back of my neck, keeping my face pinned to him as he turned to face the unknown woman.

"Don't be a killjoy."

"There are dozens of other people here to corrupt."

"Fine. Have your fun," the woman said, and I could hear the sound of her heels clicking away from us.

Neither of us immediately said anything or even moved. I clung to him. He held me to his body.

I'd embraced many women in my life. It had always been nice and comforting.

But this?

This was something new entirely. Something that was both nice and comforting, but managed to be other things as well. Like exciting. And it, oddly, made me somehow feel very small and very protected.

Protected.

In the arms of a demon.

It made no sense.

But there was also no denying that was how it felt, either.

"Think you're done here," Ace's voice said, making the both of us stiffen, but there didn't appear to be anything in his voice that suggested he knew it was me that was clinging to Ly. "There's work to be done," he added before walking off.

Those words seemed to break through whatever emotion had allowed Ly to hold onto me.

He all but flung me away from him.

I flew backward, nearly slamming into the wall with the sudden lack of his strength holding me up.

"Go back to watching people fuck," he told me, something coming down over his face, masking anything real. It was a hard and cold mask, making a shiver course through me. "And don't fucking talk to anyone. Don't make me regret letting you be here, witch," he said, turning on his heel and storming away.

Alone, I fell back against the wall, feeling a sudden need to pull the jacket closed in the front, cover up, hide away.

I wasn't familiar with the sensations assaulting my system all at once. But they were reminiscent of sadness, of rejection, of confusion, and of shame.

"You okay?" a female voice asked at my side, making me turn to find a pretty, petite blonde-haired, green-eyed woman standing there in jeans and a loose-fitting sage green shirt, an outfit that seemed out of place in this home full of near-nakedness. Including, it seemed, my own.

It was right then that I realized there was wetness on my cheek, that I had tears flooding my vision.

"I don't know," I admitted, shaking my head, reaching up with one hand to wipe at my cheeks as the other held the front of my jacket closed.

"They're bastards, every one of them," she declared, the vehemence in her voice making me wonder if she had personal experience with their wickedness. "Even the woman."

"Red," I recalled Ly calling her.

"Yeah, Red. She's just as bad but in a different way. Did they hurt you?"

That wasn't an easy question to answer.

Yes and no.

Daily.

And who knew what was to come?

That said, I didn't think any of that was what this woman meant. She meant in the way men could sometimes hurt a woman. When she was unwilling and he refused to respect that.

"No. I just... that shouldn't have happened, is all," I admitted, feeling the heat rise in my cheeks at the idea of anyone watching what Lycus did to me like I had watched other couples during this party.

"They make things that shouldn't happen, happen a lot," the woman said, voice tense, words dripping with vitriol. "I'm Dale," she said, reaching her hand out toward me.

I wasn't supposed to talk to anyone. That was the rule. That said, Ly was nowhere to be seen, and I doubted this woman would tattle on me.

So I slid my hand into hers. "Lenore."

"Pretty. Anyway... don't worry, Lenore. I am going to take every last one of those dem—assholes down," she vowed before walking away, and then right out the front door.

Demons.

She was going to say demons, right?

I hadn't been imagining that.

She'd caught herself at the last second, but she was absolutely going to say demons.

Which meant... what?

It had to mean something.

Since humans didn't believe in demons, not really, not in the literal way. Or if they did, they believed they lived in hell only, or that they did things like possess individuals.

They didn't believe demons walked around wearing the handsome faces of motorcycle-riding men.

So, that meant that this woman, Dale, knew something. Did that make her some sort of witch? I didn't get that feeling from her, that sizzle of connection I felt with my coven. But maybe that had something to do with the fact that she wasn't part of my coven. I knew nothing about other witches. Surely, ours wasn't the only coven. And if other witches didn't live in the woods like we did, perhaps they would walk around the world just like the normal people did.

Maybe they plotted to send the demons back to hell.

How, I had no idea. Since the reason the coven had agreed to the treaty all those years ago was because the demons had proven unkillable, forever stuck on this human plane.

But maybe other witches, modern witches, knew more than we did. Perhaps there was a way to send them all back to hell for good.

I should have been thrilled at the prospect.

Why, then, was there a strange sinking sensation in my chest at the very idea?

This was just all too much, I decided, looking around.

The whole party came rushing back. The thumping of the music, the clash of voices, the shouts and curses as well as all the sights.

Where it had been exciting and fascinating, it now felt overwhelming and ugly.

Stomach twisting hard enough that I felt nausea rise up my throat, I pulled my shoulders up toward my ears, ducked my head, and rushed through the house, escaping into the kitchen, trying to open the door, but finding it locked.

There was no key in sight.

I guess one of the demons—likely Minos—had locked it, assuming I was down there, not wanting any of the party guests to come down and see me.

A small, petty, selfish part of me said to run. No one would see me, or stop me. It was perhaps the only time I could get away with it.

But the other part knew someone would have to pay for it.

Another witch from my coven.

I couldn't put this curse on her, force her into my shoes.

With no other option, I turned to make my way back up to the second floor.

There were sounds from behind some of the closed doors, but this floor was otherwise unoccupied.

Feeling a small bit of relief, I rushed into Ly's room, slamming, and locking the door before rushing into the bathroom.

I stripped out of the new clothes, feeling suddenly like they were burning my skin, like they were an ugly costume I had been wearing all evening, maybe partially responsible for what had happened.

Back in my own gown, I grabbed a cloth and scrubbed at my face with soap and water until all traces of the other version of me were erased from my reflection.

Finished with that, I gathered my long hair and set to carefully braiding it until the woman staring back at me was someone I recognized, even if the hollow look in her eyes was new.

It was okay.

It would all be okay.

As soon as the party was over, Minos would unlock the basement door. Then I could slip back down there.

Then I would *stay* there.

No more demanding to be a part of the inner workings of this wicked household.

I turned, going toward the bedroom, but my stomach dropped at the idea of being in bed with Ly after what happened, after his brush-off afterward.

Taking a deep breath, I gathered the extra blanket from the bed as well as a towel, moving into the massive tub instead, using it as a makeshift bed.

Hidden, protected, I felt myself drifting off to sleep more quickly than I would have thought.

"The fuck is this shit?" Ly's voice growled, shocking me awake, legs shooting out, spine straightening. All at once. Forgetting about the confines of my bed. My feet and the top of my head slammed into the unyielding porcelain, sending pain through me as my heart hammered in my chest.

"Ow ow ow," I whimpered, my hands going to the top of my head, trying to rub the ache away.

"What the fuck are you doing in the tub?" he demanded as a headache started to pound behind my eyes, the top of my head still throbbing.

"Leave me alone," I demanded, hearing a whine in my voice, hating it there.

"Get the fuck out of there," he demanded.

"I wouldn't be here if the basement wasn't locked," I shot back, anger replacing the surge of sadness I had felt a moment before.

"There's a bed in the other room," he reminded me as though I was too stupid to remember that fact. "Get out," he tried again, reaching down to grab my hand, to pull it away from the top of my head.

And the rage that poured through me sizzled, and zapped at the point of contact between our bodies.

"Fuck," Ly hissed, yanking his hand away as I shot upward.

My mother could shock someone if she got angry. I always figured it was unique to her. But, apparently, it was a family trait. I had just never been angry enough to see it manifest.

The shock on Ly's face as he cradled his hand to his chest matched the sensation I felt inside.

Because, suddenly, I didn't feel quite as powerless.

I might have been forced to live in this house, to be a Sacrifice to this group of evil creatures.

But that didn't mean I was weak.

It didn't mean I had to accept abuse from them.

"Don't grab at me," I told him, angling my chin upward, faking a fierceness I in no way felt.

"No shit," he shot back, pulling his arm out to inspect his hand.

It was bloodshot and blistered, a raw-looking wound I knew wouldn't last.

You couldn't kill demons.

You could wound them.

But only temporarily.

And then you would need to deal with their anger afterward.

"Look at me," Ly demanded, drawing my gaze up from his raw hand. "Don't tell Ace you can do that."

"Why not?" I asked, wanting to shout it from the rooftops, needing everyone to know I wasn't weak.

"Trust me."

"Why would I ever do that?" I shot back, feeling my lower lip start to tremble before I forced it to toughen up.

"You might not like me, witch. But I can fucking guarantee that you won't like it if any of the others find out you can do that."

I didn't know what he meant. I didn't want to ask. But there was something in his tone that told me he wasn't lying to me.

The others could never figure out that I could do more than make it rain when I was sad.

"Get out of the tub," he demanded again, glancing at his hand which already looked less red.

Because it was my plan, I climbed out of the tub, moved past Ly, then through his room, to the door.

"Where do you think you're going?" Ly hissed at me as I stepped into the hall.

"Back to the basement."

"I didn't say you had to go," he shot back.

"No," I agreed, turning to look at him. "But I want to."

"And if I said you can't go?" he said, brow raising, clearly not used to being argued with.

"I'd wonder if you were able to stop me," I told him, chin jerking up as I raised my hand, rubbing my fingertips together. It was all for show. I felt nothing, no sizzle of power, but he didn't know that.

To that, his eyes went hard.

"Be very fucking careful," Ly said, teeth clenched as he tried to speak through them. "You don't want to fuck with me, witch."

"Maybe *you* don't want to *fuck* with me." The words felt clumsy on my lips, but came out strong.

And while I still felt like I had the upper hand, I made my way slowly down the hall, the stairs, and into the unlocked basement.

Chapter Eight

Lycus

She was powerful.

I should have been happy about that, excited, even.

It was good for us.

It was what we had been looking for with the coven for generations.

It was what we had been missing.

It might make all the difference.

But I'd told her not to tell anyone.

It made no fucking sense.

I stood in my bedroom an hour later, watching the color start to return to my hand, the blisters shrinking and disappearing like they'd never been there in the first place.

One second of contact to her power had given me third degree burns. I shouldn't have been able to burn. Not when I came from a place where everything burned. But she had done it to me.

That was the kind of power that could change everything.

I guess she wasn't the reject she believed herself to be.

And, I imagined, her coven had no idea they'd sent us the most powerful witch we'd seen in generations.

I should have been running from my room to find Ace to tell him, to share this new information and discuss all the ways it might change everything forever for us.

We should have all been gathering in the study to have a drink, toasting to the end of all our troubles.

But, no.

I'd told her to keep it to herself.

I planned to keep it to myself.

It made no sense.

It was disloyal.

And it would all be for nothing, because, eventually, they were all going to find out.

Then, well, I had no idea.

I wasn't exactly doing Lenore a kindness by keeping her secret. I was, at best, just buying her more time to be a prisoner in our home.

That said, a prisoner was likely better than what may lay ahead for her if the truth got out.

I went ahead and had that drink, though it wasn't for celebration, but rather guilt that needed drowning.

The sun was high in the sky before I finally climbed into my bed.

All in all, the party was a success. We'd done what we all set out to do. It was maybe the wildest of all our parties, in fact.

I should have been focusing on that.

Instead, my mind was plagued with other thoughts.

A short skirt.

No panties.

The heady, sweet smell of her.

The feel of her tight pussy pulsating around my fingers.

The sound of my name on her lips as she came.

My cock was rock-hard in seconds at the memory, pride flooding my system at the memory of her body racked with aftershocks from the power of her orgasm.

Raw and untouched; that was what the witch was.

Innocence had never been appealing to me before.

Corruption was fun, of course, stoking that baseness in all human beings. But virgins were too easy. The challenge was more fun. Besides, what I did for work, and what I enjoyed personally, physically, were different things.

I'd fucked a virgin or two in my day, but a long, long time ago. Back before I realized that it wasn't as fun as fucking someone who knew what they were doing, who sucked like a porn star, begged for what they wanted, and could take a dick without crying about it.

Virgins weren't my fetish.

I avoided them completely.

And yet...

"Fuck," I hissed, reaching down to free my cock, stroking it to the memory of how openly the witch had responded to me, the sounds she made, the way her fingers clawed at me.

I came faster than a guy first touching his junk.

Harder, even.

Leaving me no less aching after I cleaned up and got ready for bed.

Shit was getting too fucking complicated.

The witch.

My reaction to her.

The way she said jump and I leapt.

Giving her a garden.

Letting her cook.

Buying her clothes and girl shit.

Allowing her to join the party.

Touching her.

Then fucking telling her to keep her powers secret.

What the fuck was going on with me?

Whatever it was, it had to stop. And for that to happen, I guess I needed to stay away from the witch.

Apparently, though, it would be easier said than done.

Chapter Nine

Lenore

"Witch?" a voice called, making me jolt out of my daydream.

In my mind, I had drifted back to Yule—the winter solstice—celebration with my coven. I had always enjoyed the colder seasons best.

In the days leading up to Yule, we would gather pinecones, would make garlands to frame the doors. We would bake sweet treats, and make homemade gifts for one another.

My mother always knitted new cold weather items—shawls, mittens, scarves, thick socks.

I had always found my fingers clumsy with needles.

But I had always been rather good with art.

Each year, I would dedicate myself to designing one new card to a deck of oracle cards I created, giving each person closest to me a new one. I had been working on them since I was fifteen.

I guessed, now, the deck would never be completed.

My heart ached at the idea of my mother's face not lighting up as she unwrapped the linen I would put it in, running her finger lovingly over the picture, asking me what the image stood for, how she would interpret it in an oracle reading.

Someone else would step in to make sure my mother wasn't alone for the holiday. They would have her in their homes, and would give her gifts. She would be taken care of.

That was a comfort, of sorts.

My heart hammered hard in my chest as I folded up in bed, realizing the voice didn't belong to Lycus. Or Ace. Or Drex. Not even the woman from the night of the party, Red.

No.

This was someone I hadn't met yet.

And with that came new worries.

About their intentions.

"Go away," I demanded, grabbing the blanket off the bed, holding it in front of me.

"Witch," the voice rumbled again, boots coming down the last few steps, making their way around, into the light from the window, revealing one of the men I had seen at the parties, a profile I had caught once or twice coming down the stairs before.

Minos.

He was handsome in a different way than Ly with his long hair, half pulled up and wrapped into a bun, and his facial hair, extremely tall body, and well-defined muscles.

There was something cold in his eyes, despite the hint of red I came to recognize in all the demons.

"Go away," I demanded again, yanking the blanket higher, holding it under my chin.

"Trust me, that is of no interest to me," he rumbled at me in a voice that sounded like gravel.

"What do you want?" I asked.

To that, his brow raised. As did his arms, making my gaze fall to see the tray there. "You haven't been upstairs for three days."

Had it been that long?

I spent the whole first day after the party asleep, finding myself tired down to my bones. The day after that, I wallowed. And this day, I daydreamed so deeply that I felt none of the calls of my body.

But now that Minos mentioned it, my stomach felt knotted and angry with its emptiness.

"You can sulk all you want, but you have to eat."

"If I don't, will you force-feed me?" I shot back, getting a little sick of these demons bossing me around.

"That shit is up for Ace to decide. I bring the food. That's what I do. You eat it, you don't, not my problem. Though, I was told to stop bringing you *flesh*, so I did that."

He made his way to the bed, dropping the tray onto my lap.

There was an odd array of foods arranged there. Carrot and celery slices with some sort of white dip, raspberries, slices of plain rye bread, and a small bowl of almonds and walnuts.

The vegetables and fruit were new.

Someone had been to the store to pick them up for me since my garden wasn't producing yet, and the last time I had been in the kitchen, there hadn't been any of it in the refrigerator.

"I forgot the tea," Minos said, shaking his head.

"You made me tea?"

"No."

"Ly?" I asked, his name a bittersweet thing on my tongue.

"Why he wouldn't bring it the fuck down himself is beyond me," Minos said, sighing.

"I heard Drex say you always feed us."

"No one else would remember," Minos admitted, shaking his head. "Except, apparently, Lycus. But only this generation," he said, eyes probing, making assumptions, coming to conclusions. "Are you coming upstairs today?"

"No."

"Tomorrow?"

"*No*."

Minos watched me for a long second before shrugging.

"Suit yourself."

"You're judging me."

"If you have freedom, and you don't use it, you're a fucking idiot," he told me, then turned away, making his way back up the steps.

Alone, I tore into the food, finishing everything provided to me, but feeling famished even after.

I tried to convince myself it was enough, that I would get fed again soon, and that I could stay where I was and tolerate a little hunger.

In the end, the desire for more food—especially that interesting dip—overtook me.

I inched my way up the stairs, stopping at the top, listening at the door for a long moment. When I was sure no one was there, I rushed out, making a beeline for the refrigerator, finding more carrots and celery, and a bottle of something that said "ranch" on the front that appeared to be the interesting dip.

"You're fucking stubborn," Ly's voice said, making me whip around, a gasp escaping me as I spun to find him standing in the doorway to the front of the house.

He looked even better than he did in the explicit dreams that plagued me when I closed my eyes. In those dreams, he was behind me, inside me, touching me the same way the man had been touching the woman at the party.

Feeling my body start to respond to him, I ducked my head and made my way toward the basement door.

"Not so fast, witch," he said, moving across the room in a few strides, blocking my retreat.

"Don't touch me," I snapped, voice coming out sharp, shrill. And I could only hope he took it as a warning.

"If I remember correctly," he said, voice silky, "you like it when I touch you."

"Hey now, what do we have here?" a female voice asked, heels clicking as she walked into the room.

Ly's eyes closed for a second at her voice, taking a steadying breath, like her presence was putting a crimp in his plans.

Turning, I found the woman who I'd heard at the party. The one named Red. Which was a fitting name, given her hair.

I wondered while looking at her how any man could see her and not realize she couldn't possibly be human. She was too perfect, too beautiful.

There were many beautiful women in my coven.

Mother nature shaped us all in unique ways.

And since there was no competition for men, there was no reason to feel anything about another woman's beauty.

Standing here, though, I couldn't help but wonder if Lycus and Red were ever an item, if he touched her the way he'd touched me, if he liked it more.

Envy was an ugly trait, one of the few emotions that the coven actively discouraged. All the others, from the positive ones like joy and hope to the negative like sadness and anger, were all accepted expressions of our inner world.

Envy was something unnatural, something born of resentment and feelings of lacking.

There was no denying that was the feeling curling its ugly fingers around my heart, though.

"The Sacrifice," I supplied, lifting my chin a bit as her eyes moved over me. Whether she found me lacking or not was beyond me, though.

"Oh, is it that time again?" she mused, perfectly arched brows pinching. "I'm a little rusty, Lycus, but since when do the witches roam around the house?"

"Since they make it rain when they're sad," he grumbled at her.

"Oh, oh that's rich," Red said, smiling. "Ace must *love* that."

"Exactly. That is why she gets to gather food and fuck around in the garden. Keeps the rain at bay."

"Well, what's her name?" Red asked, glancing at me, then Ly.

"*My* name is Lenore," I supplied. "Though everyone here seems to enjoy calling me *witch*, as though it is my name."

"Oh, I like her," she said to Ly. "I like you," she added to me. "That spirit. That has to be a good sign."

"A good sign of what?" I asked, feeling a sizzle of electricity at the base of my spine, an omen of sorts, my intuition telling me Red didn't like my spirit because she would enjoy conversation with me. Rather, my spirit might be useful to them all in some way.

But what way?

That was the question.

That was what my mind needed to be on, not ridiculous fantasies about Lycus and his hands and his mouth and, well, other things about him.

What did they want to do with me?

What was my purpose?

Why only one Sacrifice per generation?

"Of things," Red supplied, a guard going down over her face, making it clear that I wouldn't be getting anything out of her. "Ace wants us ready in ten," she added, giving Ly her attention again. "Lock up the witch, find your cut, and let's go."

With that, she was gone, heels clicking down the hall then up the stairs.

"Are you leaving for long? Should I find more food before you lock me downstairs?" I asked, angling my head to the side.

"Seeing as you willfully didn't eat for nearly three days, you should be fine," he said, yanking the door open.

The words bubbled up, angry and childish, but ultimately unstoppable.

"I hate you."

"Good," he agreed, slamming the door in my face.

He stormed off after, completely forgetting to lock the door.

I sat there on the steps, waiting, listening.

Ace, ever the whip-bearing and punctual leader, called the lingering Drex and Seven. A moment later, the rumble of their motorcycles droned off into the distance.

I waited half an hour, maybe more, before I put down my snacks and opened the door.

I made my way through the first level, then the second, making sure there was no one around.

Then, heart hammering, I went back into Ace's room.

The house, as a whole, was kept orderly. For a bunch of demons who likely didn't know how to use a broom and mop, that is. But Ace's bedroom was a mess. Not of discarded food or dirty clothing, but rather books and notebooks, scraps of paper full of cryptic phrases, charts, and maps.

He wasn't crazy, surely, but there was a lot to suggest he was obsessed.

With what, was the question.

The maps seemed to be of this general area, with certain spaces circled in red marker.

A path through the woods, following a river to what seemed like a massive rock formation had a red circle was the map closest to the top, all the others beneath had x's drawn through the circles, places investigated before.

Looking for what, though?

I shifted the maps to the side, reaching instead for the other pages.

Pages in books, notes scribbled in the margins.

About witches.

About powers.

About spells.

That was why they wanted us.

They wanted to use our powers.

To what? Find something? Tracking things wasn't exactly a strength of ours. Unless, perhaps, it was something that had belonged to us in the first place.

To sense places of power?

We could do that.

But to what end?

Demons couldn't harness power.

Their only power lay in persuasion on the human realm and eternal torture in hell.

I had more questions than answers, but my fate lay in the discovery of those conclusions.

What did they mean to do with me?

I sorted through the rest of the pages, finding nothing of significance, but took the map with me as I made my way back through the house, grabbing my cloak as well as the shoes I had worn on the trip from my coven.

And then I did the unthinkable.

I left the house.

Pulling the map out of my pocket, I moved into the woods surrounding the house, intent on finding the red circle, seeing what I might be able to deduce by being near it.

I underestimated the woods, though, misinterpreted the simplicity of the map.

I'd always been good with direction. You could have dropped me off in any random spot in the woods around my home, and I would have found my way back.

But as the minutes turned to hours, as my thighs burned, and my breath heaved as I scaled hill after hill, I realized I wasn't as adept as I had once thought myself to be.

And before long, I lost sight of the estate, got so turned around that I found myself good and lost.

In the woods.

As the sun went down.

I wasn't afraid of the woods, of the dark. I was raised in them. I knew all their secrets.

My fear was of being in the woods at night had nothing to do with the woods. And everything to do with that massive estate, and with its empty basement.

And the motorcycles I'd heard returning half an hour before.

It was too late to prevent my escape's discovery, though, I reminded myself as I sat down on a fallen tree, taking a deep breath, trying to stay calm. *Getting upset about what might happen did nothing but steal the peace from the present moment.*

Marianne had always said that. I was disappointed in myself that it took so long to truly understand the meaning of those words. I guess I had simply never had much to fret about in the past. Now, though, my entire world was uncertain; my fate was dependent upon creatures known for their utter lack of mercy.

And I had gone ahead and ticked off the only one of them who seemed to—at least on occasion—have a fondness for me. I should have been using that to my advantage, not trying to push him away.

Now, he was likely going to be in trouble for my escape. Which meant there was very little chance of him being kind to me again in the future.

"Enough," I whispered to myself, shaking my head.

I took three slow, deep breaths, expanding my belly, holding, then releasing as I let the sounds of the woods greet me. The chirps of the crickets, the sounds of the frogs in the water, the rustling of the crispy leaves in the trees, the occasional skittering of some small forest creature—mice, opossums, raccoons. The hoot of an owl somewhere far off reminded me of home so deeply my heart hurt.

Before I could even tell myself to be calm, to think of happy things, the rain was pelting down, fast, unrelenting, drenching me through in a few short moments, making an already miserable day that much worse.

Unable to pull it together, I climbed under the closest tree with the fullest canopy for minimal protection from the fat drops of water as I curled up on my side in a bed of dry leaves and pine needles, brought my hands up to my face, and let it out.

I was never going to stop the rain until I exorcised all the negative emotions swirling through my system at a break-neck pace.

So I let it out.

I cried in a way I couldn't remember doing since I was a little girl.

I cried loudly, wailing, when the sounds rose up in my throat and begged for escape. My body jolted with the sobs as I used the soaked sleeve of my cloak to wipe at my eyes, then nose, only to be overcome with another wave of misery, of helplessness.

I don't know how long I lie there, but my chest felt achy, my face raw from my tears.

And then, it happened.

A nudge.

A ridiculous surge of hope swelled within me.

Lycus.

He'd come—even through the torrential downpour—to bring me back.

My eyes fluttered open, finding my lids swollen, squeezing my eyes into slits.

Which was what I blamed the image on at first.

Tired, tear-puffy eyes.

Because, surely, that was the only thing that made any sense.

There was no way a massive wolf was standing before me.

Wolves weren't even native to this area, as far as I could remember. Coyotes, yes. Wolves, no.

But even as my eyes adjusted and the rain suddenly stopped, when fear—instead of sadness—became my prevailing emotion, and the moon and stars shone through the sparse canopy of trees, there was no denying it.

This was a wolf.

A pure black wolf.

With big yellow eyes.

Staring right at me.

I'd never seen a wolf in person before, but, surely, this one was larger than usual. He was beast-like, more bear-sized than wolf-sized, towering over me, his massive paws bigger than a man's hand in the mud at my side.

"Good puppy," I cooed at it. When in doubt, I found soothing baby animal voices did wonders, even on predators you may run across in your travels. "That's a good puppy," I added, my gaze averting, head ducking, but keeping it in my peripheral as I slowly raised a hand, closing around my own throat, wanting to protect my most vulnerable spot. "That's a good puppy. I'm not going to hurt you, so you don't hurt me, okay?" I asked, trying to convince myself to stay calm, knowing dogs could sense that kind of thing.

But there was no use pretending I wasn't terrified when I felt massive, sharp teeth dig into the wrist of my hand at my throat pulling me to my feet, until I as following dumbly behind the giant beast lest his teeth sink further in.

I could feel a trickle down my hand, and I couldn't tell if it was his saliva, my blood, or a combination of the two as he pulled me through the woods alongside him, seeming to have a destination in mind.

Where?

To his pack? So they could all enjoy eating me alive?

My stomach flipped, sending the food I had eaten earlier up my throat, needing to swallow hard to force it back down.

Maybe I should have fought. Surely, I stood more of a chance of surviving trying to fight off a lone wolf instead of an entire pack of them, but a small part of me was clinging to hope that maybe it didn't intend to kill me.

Could it be possible that it was a pet wolf? A massive pet wolf. Who was bringing me home to his master?

That was what I was trying to convince myself as it picked up the pace into a trot, expecting me to keep up even though he had a two-leg advantage on me.

Sweat poured as we kept the breakneck pace. I lost a shoe, felt the bottom of that foot getting chewed up by twigs and rocks and brambles, but was unable to pull to a stop because anytime I did, those huge teeth just sank deeper.

The metallic note of blood met my palate as the never-ending trek led us up a steep incline, causing my thighs to scream, my lungs hurt.

Then, just when I was sure I couldn't take anymore, the wolf slowed, puffing out his breath through his nostrils, then pulling me into a giant rock formation, down into the cavern-like depths.

There, deep inside, his teeth released my wrist. His massive head whacked into me, shoving me in another couple of feet as he huffed again, turned in a circle, and lay down in the opening to the only exit.

With nothing else to do, I slid down the wall, cradling my wrist to my chest, pulling my wounded foot up onto my other thigh, taking deep breaths, trying not to cry out.

The wolf's gaze pinned me, but he made no move to attack, to do anything but stare at me with the oddly knowing eyes of his.

Then I heard it.

A howl, far off in the distance.

Followed by another. Then another. And another.

Until, finally, my wolf threw his head back and joined in, the sound so loud it made my ears ring.

Dread filled my belly as I kept hearing these calls, answered by my wolf, getting closer and closer with each passing moment.

They were coming.

To see what their friend had found.

And I was a sitting duck with bleeding wounds.

I had no idea what fate lay ahead of me with the demons, but I was pretty sure it would be preferable to being torn apart by wild wolves.

But pretty soon, the howls stopped.

Because I could hear the distinct tap-tap-tap sound of giant claws on the rock floor.

They were coming...

Chapter Ten

Lycus

She was gone.

My stomach plummeted at that realization when we made it home later that evening after going to a local MC meet-up, networking, handing out product, trading it for different kinds, building our stockpile for the next party that was already being planned.

"Fuck!" I roared, grabbing the edge of her nightstand, flipping it up, flinging it against the wall, feeling the Change taking over me, not even bothering to try to control it.

"What the fuck is going on?" Ace called, running down the steps. One look at me, in nearly my complete True Form, with the nightstand tossed and broken, and Ace's eyes were blazing red too. "She got away?" he asked, his fingers stretching into talons.

His having been around much longer than the rest of us, it was rare to see Ace lose control of the Change. Even when his temper flared, you never so much as saw the red overtake his eyes. He controlled it.

Except for now.

Because of my fuck-up.

Because I had been in a pissy-ass mood with the witch, and left in a rush without making sure to lock the door when I knew none of us would be around to keep an eye on her.

"Damn it," he roared, tearing back up the stairs, calling out for the others.

Ace, whether he had shared it with the rest of us or not, clearly had a good feeling about this witch. He'd never given a shit about the others, always seemed to know the moment they arrived that they weren't exactly what we were looking for. He would use them all the same, but it was like he was going through the motions.

He thought Lenore was something special.

He thought she might have been the one we had been waiting for.

He thought she was our only hope.

And now she was gone.

Fuck.

I tore up the stairs as well, finding the others gathered around, casting anxious glances at our leader as he paced, the change flickering in and out in its intensity, something wild to see.

"Aram and I will take off on our bikes, track the roads," Red suggested, ready to spring into action.

"It rained," I murmured, looking out at the droplets on the windows.

"We will go to the coven," Drex added. "Get another one."

"It rained," I said again, getting ignored. "Hey!" I yelled, making Ace turn, pinning me with his red eyes. "Ace, it rained," I told him, trying to make him understand, not sure how rational he was being in the moment. "Just around this area. Remember? On the way in, it was dry except down this street. She made it rain. She's somewhere and she was upset about it. It has to be the woods," I added, looking out the darkened back window.

"Go," Ace demanded, back to pacing.

I didn't need more than that.

I turned and I was running, vaguely aware of Minos breaking into the woods about the same time I did, but the two of us taking off in different directions.

I didn't think she ran away, not really.

She didn't want to have another member of her coven have to take her place because she was a chickenshit. Knowing her, she got a wild hair, and wanted to take a walk in the woods to remind herself of her home. And then she got lost. Or hurt.

Fuck.

Why was there an aching sensation in my chest at the idea of the latter?

It shouldn't have mattered to me if she was lost in the woods and wounded. If anything, it would have made her easier to find.

But it mattered.

I cared.

My heart was thudding against my ribcage at the idea of her being prone, and some predator coming upon her. Bear were especially ravenous this time of year, gearing up for hibernation. And while black bears didn't typically eat humans, you never really knew, did you?

I stopped a few yards into the woods, closing my eyes, taking a deep breath, allowing the anger at myself, at this situation, at something potentially happening to her overtake me.

The Change came upon me faster than ever before, horns tearing through my temples, talons shooting through my fingertips. My senses honed in, making the dark woods seem brighter, the sounds crisper, the scents sharper.

Inhaling deep, I found the lingering traces of ripe fruit, a smell I knew only belonged to Lenore.

Then I was running.

Following the creek at first, then inexplicably going uphill.

Where she thought she was going, I had no idea. I didn't pretend to understand witches. Maybe she had some kind of sixth sense about an animal in danger, or some fucking herb was growing wild that she wanted to pick, or some other shit. Who knew.

But doing stupid shit like that would explain how she got so lost so quickly, and was upset enough to make it start raining.

Sure, she'd grown up in the woods, isolated from everything. But those were *her* woods. She knew the trees there, the paths home, how to find food, and water, and protection. She didn't have any of those advantages here.

And if she got hurt on top of that, that would sure explain why the ground was sopping wet, my boots slogging through slippery, thick mud as I followed the scent of her deeper and deeper into the woods.

I was faster than she would have been, taking off at a dead run, but also being longer-legged, and more powerful, but she must have been walking for hours before she came to a stop in the spot I was closing in on, her scent stronger there, though not strong enough that she was still there.

As I got closer, though, my stomach clenched hard.

Because it wasn't just the sweet scent of fruit there.

Oh, no.

There was the coppery scent of blood.

"Fuck," I hissed, pushing through the last few yards, finding a downed tree and a human-sized imprint in the mud beside it.

She'd been laying there during the rain.

And then something had made her bleed.

Night vision nowhere near as good as my day vision, even with the Change, I reached for my phone, turning on the flashlight, and looking around.

I saw nothing for a long moment.

And then...

"Fuck," I yelled, raking my hand through my hair, forgetting about the talons, feeling them ripping across my scalp. But I barely noted the pain as my mind raced, and I tried to figure out my move.

Every ounce of me wanted to follow the bloody trail, wanted to find her, save her.

But a very small, still rational part of me understood something else.

I couldn't do it alone.

I scrolled through my contacts to make a call to Ace as I started running back, but the woods were shit for reception, so I gave up, pushing my legs harder, ignoring the burn in my lungs as I called out for Minos as I got closer toward the property.

He appeared out of the tree-line almost at the same time, just as rundown, half-Changed, and eyes wild.

"What is it?" he asked, following me inside as I called for Ace.

"What?" Ace asked, mostly Changed back, but his eyes were still red, and there were small points of his horns in his forehead. "What is it?"

"They have her," I gasped out, trying to catch my breath enough to get more words out.

"Who?" Ace demanded. "Who has her?"

"I saw tracks," I added, taking a slow, deep breath.

"Fucking tell me who has her, Lycus," Ace snapped.

"The shifters," I told him, shaking my head, seeing the dread cross his face as it had crossed my heart and mind back in the woods. "The shifters have her."

Chapter Eleven

Lenore

There were a dozen of them in all once they all came in, all different colors from black and brown, to brindle, to sandy, to pure white. All their eyes were different colors as well, practically glowing in the dark.

Their thick coats reeked of wet dog as they filed in, forming a semi-circle around me, noses in the air, taking deep sniffs, but not making moves toward me as I pulled my knees into my chest, wrapped my arms around my legs protectively in case of an attack.

There was next to no movement from them for a long while, save for the sniffing and the occasional whining noise.

Then the white one moved toward the center of the circle, head tipping to the side as it looked at me, then slowly inched its way closer. Almost, if it was possible for a predator to do so, carefully, as if not to spook me.

It walked up, sticking its big wet nose in my face, my hair, over my injured hand, then foot, then turned away, letting out a huffing sound, and moving to sit in the center of the semi-circle.

This was some unspoken wolf-conversation because, one by one, the other wolves did the exact same thing, each inspecting me, seeming to be looking for something about me, but none appeared to find what they were looking for, giving up to go lie down back in their places in the semi-circle.

After the last wolf moved away, the massive white one in the center, letting out his own huff, rolled his head around, much the way a person would to remove a crick.

Then, as it leapt to a kneel, it seemed to explode into the air, replaced instead with the form of a man, tall, incredibly muscular, sweaty, blond-haired, blue-eyed, with a massive scar down the side of his face.

And stark freaking naked.

I didn't want to look, but from my position, when I glanced up, there it all was, hanging out. Big and commanding but not, it seemed, interested in me.

Small miracles, I guess.

I probably should have been shocked. To see a wolf turn into a man. But there had been tales of shifters in even the most ancient of our holy texts. True, over time, we had mostly relegated them to the same sort of thing as fairy tales, but to have those old stories proven true wasn't as shocking as coming upon an actual shifter with no prior knowledge of them would have been.

The transition itself was magnificent, made all my powers seem small in comparison, but I wasn't sitting there disbelieving my eyes.

If anything, I was racking my brain to try to remember what the stories said about shifters, their loyalties, and their feelings toward my kind.

But, in the moment, I was coming up all blank.

"It has been a long time since I've seen a witch," the white wolf declared, voice sounding rough. Whether that was his natural voice, or his throat was raw from the earlier howling, was anyone's guess. "I was starting to think you'd all died out." I couldn't seem to force my mouth to say anything to that. Part of me was scared to reveal that there were still covens around, not knowing the intentions of these shifters. The other part was too scared, too tired, too hurt, to think of anything else. "You're lucky we found you. There are all kinds of bad things in these parts," he said in a way that made me think that, while he didn't know about witches, he did know about demons. And that he had some opinions about them. None of them good. "What were you doing in the woods?"

"I, ah, I was taking a walk," I told him, it being mostly the truth. "And I got lost." That was also true. He didn't need to know the motivations for the walk.

"And then got caught in that storm," the white wolf said. "It was good that Lex came across you," he went on, waving toward the big black wolf that had dragged me through the woods. "Though he could have been easier on you," he said, acknowledging my bloody hand and foot. "Come on over here and climb on," he offered, motioning to Lex's back. "It is the least he can do, to give you a lift back to our clubhouse."

He didn't exactly phrase it as though I had any kind of choice in the matter. But, still, now that I knew he was an actual human under all the fur and teeth and paws, I felt really strange at the idea of riding him like a horse.

"I can walk," I assured the leader, giving him a wobbly smile.

"Witch, it's been a long night. Just get on Lex, so we can all get home, get something to eat, then figure out what to do about you." The words weren't overly sharp, but the tone sure was, making me slowly unfold, hobbling over toward Lex, who was still lying on the ground.

There was no use trying to fight.

I was outnumbered.

They had fangs and claws.

I stood no chance.

Even if I suddenly found the anger to zap them.

So I carefully grabbed some of Lex's fur with my good hand, lifting my bad leg, and pushing it over his back, immediately sliding over.

"Got you," the white wolf said, big hand grabbing my hip, stopping me from falling—or clawing out Lex's fur. "There you go," he added, pushing me into my spot. "Legs tight like you're riding some good dick, babe," he demanded, then slapped Lex's rump, who immediately moved to stand, making my thighs tighten immediately.

"We'll take it easy," the leader declared before dropping down toward the floor, exploding back into a wolf seamlessly before he landed.

With that, everyone fell into a trot behind their leader as we made our way out of the cave and back into the woods.

We broke through the tree-line just as the sun was coming up, allowing me to watch a low, one-story structure come into view. Not so much a home, I wouldn't say, as a building. Ugly red metal walls, a flat roof with a railing, large windows.

But, it appeared, this was the clubhouse that the leader had referred to, since we were all making our way in that direction, passing a couple sets of wooden tables in the back as well as a giant fire pit, surrounded by massive tree stumps to be used as seating.

The white wolf slammed a paw into the back door, nails scratching downward, making a horrid noise that made my teeth hurt for a moment before the door was pulled open from the inside by an older gentleman, shoulders scrunched forward, giving the pack a small smile before his eyes fell on me.

"For fuck's sake, Sully," the old man said, looking over at the white wolf, the motion making the side of his neck visible, where there were four massive claw marks. "A witch? What kind of trouble are you bringing to this pack?" he added as Sully burst into human form again, as did all the other wolves. Including Lex, whose smooth human back left nothing to hold onto, leaving me spiraling backward, slamming hard on the ground, letting out a grunt, then a whimper as the pain ricocheted through my head. "Jesus Christ," the old man grumbled, throwing his hands up at the pack as he made his way toward me, extending a hand.

"We saved her, Pops," Sully said, shaking his head.

"Saved her then did nothing about her wounds, then gave her another one. Genius. The whole fucking coven will be coming down on our heads."

"Please," Sully said, shaking his head. "When was the last time you heard about a single witch, let alone a coven? We were getting her back here to take care of her foot and hand. Or would you rather us lick her wounds clean?" Sully asked before looking at me. "Come on. We'll get you cleaned up."

Having no choice, and genuinely in need of cleaning up lest I develop an infection, I followed Sully into the clubhouse.

The inside was better than the outside let on.

Sure, it was almost utilitarian in its style with the cement floors and lack of window treatments, blankets, pillows, anything soft and homey, but everything was clean and well taken care of. To the left inside the back door was a massive living room area with several couches facing a massive television. There was a long wooden dining table with at least sixteen seats. And, finally, in the main room, was a kitchen with an oversize island, cement countertops, and appliances of the silver metal I'd heard Ace refer to as stainless steel.

To the side of the kitchen was a doorway that led beyond. Bedrooms or bathrooms or storage, or all three.

"Sit," Sully demanded, pressing me into the head seat at the dining room table as he walked passed me toward the doorway, his rear muscles dancing as he went.

I glanced back around, seeing all the others filing inside, each and every one of the men stark naked still. Their light, and tan, and brown, and black skin, gleaming with sweat, was taut over powerful muscles. Every single one of them was unabashed at their nudity as they moved past me to follow Sully into the unknown space.

I'd seen more nude men in the past week than I had ever seen in my life.

I couldn't help but wonder if this was what it was like for normal, human women. If their lives were a parade of various male sex organs. Or if, perhaps, this was only happening to me.

It was also interesting to note that while each of these naked men was fantastically good-looking, well-built, powerful, and confident, not a single one of them seemed to affect me the way that Lycus had.

"Can I get you something to drink? Eat?" Pops asked, moving in front of me but staying a respectable distance away, making it clear he was no threat.

He was afraid of me, I noticed.

I wasn't sure anyone had ever been afraid of me before.

Even after I burned Lycus, he hadn't shown me fear. Just surprise and interest and worry.

If these shifters believed I had powers—even ones I did not possess—then that gave me an advantage. It would possibly even help secure my freedom.

You know... so I could go back and be imprisoned with the demons again.

Oh, the Gods.

What a mess my life had become.

"Something to drink would be great," I said, giving him a small smile.

"Cold or hot? We have coffee. Fresh. Get it before they all pounce on it."

I didn't want coffee. I didn't like coffee. That said, I was exhausted from not sleeping, and I needed to be able to keep my wits about me.

"Coffee would be great."

While Pops moved to make my coffee, Sully came back out from the other end of the clubhouse, his hands full of various items. He was still nude from the waist up, but had slipped into low-slung—very low-slung—pants.

"I figured this might offend your delicate sensibilities less," he said, waving toward his pants. "Usually, women don't complain about seeing me naked, but the way I hear it, witches tend to be all about their fellow women."

I said nothing to that, not sure what there *was* to say. He was right and he was wrong. There were some witches in our coven who enjoyed the company of other women in more carnal ways, but not all, not even most. We simply believed that being without men and the complications they often brought on, made us more powerful.

"Hand," he demanded, squatting down in front of me, reaching for a plastic bottle, and squeezing some of the liquid onto a fluff of cotton.

I thought nothing of it, holding out my hand toward him, until he touched me, and the pain shot through my cuts and up my arm.

The surprise of it, the shocked anger of my body, had the sizzle starting, uncontrollable, making Sully curse and yank backward, holding onto his hand, eyes wide.

"What happened?"

"She shocked me," Sully said, then shook his head as he looked down at his hand. "No," he corrected. "She burned me. What the fuck?" he asked, looking at me, brows drawn together.

"I told you not to mess with a witch," Pops said, bringing my coffee over, but being very careful not to so much as brush me as he put it down on the table.

"I didn't expect for your ministrations to burn that much," I told Sully, feeling apologeticI didn't let that slip into my tone, wanting to seem strong, confident, like my powers weren't a surprise to me, but rather a natural reaction to pain being inflicted upon me.

"It's alcohol. It burns," Sully informed me, reaching to show me the bottle.

"I understand that now. We don't use alcohol in my coven. I can clean the wound myself now that I have the items," I told them, gritting my teeth so I didn't cry out while I cleaned my hand then my foot with the wretched alcohol. "This cream," I said, waving it at Sully. "This will work as a salve?"

"Salve. Christ. I need a drink for this," Sully declared, turning to walk away toward a cabinet in the living room, pulling a bottle of amber liquid out, the same stuff Drex liked to drink so much.

"Yes," Pops said, motioning to the tube of cream. "That will work as a salve. Prevent infection. But you are going to want to wrap your feet up. Those cuts are deep. You could leave your hand out. I will have a word with Lex about biting pretty girls he saves in the woods."

"I probably pulled his fur pretty hard on the way here, so I can't be too mad about it," I said, shrugging, as I slathered the cream onto my hand with another cotton puff, then carefully did the same to my foot.

"Here, do you want some help?" Pops asked when I tried to wrap my foot.

"She's not a child, Pops," Sully objected.

"No, but she is a lady. You'll excuse these brutes," Pops said, shaking his head as he carefully took the wrap from my hand. "They haven't had a woman around here in a while. They've clearly forgotten their manners." He'd said the last part loudly, a chastisement to Sully who took another drink in response. "There now. All better. What do you say we get you something dry to wear?" he asked. "You're shivering."

I hadn't even noticed.

My head was racing too much with everything else going on to notice something so small.

"Yeah, heaven forbid she gets pneumonia," Sully agreed, snorting. "The coven might hex us all."

Pops and I both chose to ignore that as he led me back through the doorway that opened up into a hall. "They're rude," he said, shaking his head. "I try to talk manners into 'em, but they're not my boys. There's only so much I can do."

"I appreciate your kindness," I told him, offering him a small smile.

"It's nothing. Here. Through here," he said, leading me into a small room with a bed, nightstand, and dresser. "I have some clothes in here that should fit you," he said, rummaging in his dresser, pulling out a button-up shirt and a pair of sleep pants in dark gray. "I wish I had something more appropriate."

"These will be fine," I told him, already dying for something dry and warm on. And maybe something a little less feminine, a little more concealing.

"You can stay here," Pops offered. "This is my room," he added.

"I can't stay in your room."

"Sure you can. I don't need it right now. And it will allow you to get some rest. In private. While we all figure out how to get you home."

"She's not going anywhere, Pops," Sully said from the door, shaking his head.

"Your father would be rolling over in his grave," Pops growled, reaching into the bottom drawer of his dresser, pulling out a spare blanket and pillowcase, setting about making the bed.

"We burned my old man. But I get the sentiment. Doesn't change shit. Come on. She is dead on her feet," Sully said as Pops fussed with the blankets, trying to get them just so.

"Thank you again," I told him as he passed me. "I really appreciate it."

"Don't mention it," he said, but his eyes were warm as he moved into the hall, closing the door behind him.

I listened for a moment before moving to the door, carefully sliding the lock, cringing when it clicked. But no one came running.

Certain I was alone, I stripped out of my wet clothes, slipping into the new ones that hung around my body, concealing my form beneath, then grabbed my wet clothes, draping them over the foot of the bed.

I could hear the shuffling of feet down the hall and into the common space, the low timbre of male voices engaged in some sort of intense conversation.

While my weary eyes begged for the bed, my survival instinct had me rushing across the room to the small window, moving the heavy curtains to the side. My fingers had just grabbed the pull on the window when a face appeared, making me jump backward, a gasp rushing out of me.

Lex.

My supposed savior.

He was good-looking as a human like the others. Tall, fit, black-haired, dark-eyed, chiseled features. There were tattoos up and down his arms, across his neck, giving him an even more dangerous look as he gave me a head shake that said there was no escape.

Stifling a whimpering sound, I closed the curtains, climbing into the bed, curling up under the blanket Pops had provided me, and letting the helplessness sink in.

My situation wasn't much different, all things said.

I was with a group of creatures who wanted me for something.

I was being treated reasonably well.

I had no idea what my fate was.

I shouldn't have been sad. Not much had changed.

Except here, nothing was familiar.

And, of course, there was no Ly.

It was stupid that my mind went there, but it did, until the well inside that had felt drained dry the night before filled up and overflowed again.

I could hear a hissed curse outside the window as the raindrops pelted the pane.

"Not a-fucking-gain," Sully hissed from the front room.

The rest of the day was a tear-soaked blur followed by a nearly numb abyss as I lay there, waiting on my fate.

But then, out of nowhere, I could hear it.

Something familiar

Something oddly comforting.

The rumble of motorcycles.

Coming in this direction.

Ly.

Chapter Twelve

Lycus

I still felt like I could smell the wet dog scent I'd picked up on in the woods as we drove away from our estate, making our way up the hill.

We didn't know the exact location of the shifter headquarters, only that it was up in a clearing in the woods, allowing them to Shift anytime they wanted without worrying about being seen by anyone else.

It wasn't until about half an hour into the drive that I noticed something.

Rain.

On the horizon.

But concentrated in a small area.

Lenore.

That was the only explanation.

It was bright everywhere else.

I lay on my horn, getting the attention of the others, then pointing toward the sight.

Ace's tight shoulders seemed to ease a bit at having a direction, and proof that I was right about the shifters having the witch.

We knew the shifters.

Of course, we did.

We all ran in the same circles, after all.

But while we dabbled at being bikers, the shifters had been a legitimate MC for at least three generations. They dealt in anything that involved beating the shit out of people, largely working as hired muscle these days. They'd worked crowd control at a couple of the rallies we'd been to.

We had always made it a point to avoid one another.

The shifters had an ugly reputation from the beginning.

Then fucking Drex had gone ahead and stolen one of their mates from them—only for a night, mind you, but that was more than enough for them—a generation back, and shit got ugly for a couple decades.

Leadership had changed since then.

From what I'd heard, the son of the leader we'd taken out was now in charge.

And if he figured out the witch was valuable to us, who the fuck knew what he might be capable of? Just for revenge's sake.

The only thing working in our favor was that we could pay.

And they weren't exactly rolling in it. They made do. But men who made do always wanted to lighten the burden a bit. We could do that.

Ace had a lot of skills, not the least of which was figuring out how to make human money, then compound it until it was almost laughable how much he had stashed away. It wouldn't hurt our bottom line to trade for Lenore.

And since Ace had high hopes for this Sacrifice, he would pay whatever they wanted.

We pulled into the lot of their clubhouse a while later, finding it different than the last time we had seen it, when it was nothing more than a shack made of spare timber.

Whoever Junior was, he had better taste—and slightly more resources—than his old man.

At the sounds of our bikes pulling in, the front door opened and half a dozen men stepped out.

The smell of dog met my nose, something familiar and no less offensive than it had been a generation ago.

"You have something that belongs to us," Ace informed them, moving to the front.

"Yeah?" one of them asked, moving forward as well.

Even from far away, there was a resemblance to his old man. Tall, fit, blond. This was the new leader.

"Yes."

"And what makes you think that?"

"I can smell her," I declared, moving in beside Ace, who cast a quick glance at me, curious, making it clear that Lenore's scent that was so strong to me seemed lost on everyone else.

"If she is yours, what was she doing lost and upset in the woods?" another one asked, tall, dark-haired, tattooed.

"She's not that bright," Ace supplied. "She got lost while we weren't at home."

"Or was she running from you?" the leader asked, brow arching up. "A witch. I wonder what a group of demons would want with the likes of her," he mused, pinning Ace with an unwavering glare.

"We will be more than happy to make a trade," Ace offered.

"See, I know you are all rolling in it," the leader said, chin lifting. "But I can't help but wonder who else might be around who would be willing to pay more."

"She's not a fucking piece of furniture. You can't sell her," I snapped, drawing his attention.

"I think I can, actually. You want to try to stop me?" he asked, and I could feel the Change starting, my fingers elongated into talons, my horns starting to poke through my skin.

"Ly, stand down," Ace hissed at me.

"Sully," another voice called, belonging to an older man who seemed vaguely familiar in a time-drenched way. "Take the money and let the witch go. She can't bring any good here."

"Listen to your grandfather, Sully," Ace agreed, having a much better memory than I did, apparently. "No one wants another war. From the looks of things, your pack has barely recovered."

They'd been a much bigger organization once upon a time. And we'd had a big part in decimating their numbers, while not taking any real hits ourselves. They couldn't kill us, after all. Though there had been some nursing of wounds for a while after the last big fight, the one that had their leader dead, and their pack too defeated to go on.

A low growling rumbled through Sully at Ace's words, a sound imitated by his men.

"Shit," the old man hissed, sensing things coming to a fever pitch.

"No," a different voice joined the group, familiar, feminine.

I couldn't see her, hidden behind the large bodies of the shifters, but I could smell her. The sweet fruit. But mixed with something else. The tangy scent of her blood.

Another growl rumbled from Sully as he started to bend forward, something I knew from experience with the older pack preceded their shift into wolves.

"I said no!" Lenore yelled as her hand shot out, grabbing onto Sully's back as he burst into wolf form. Her fingers came into contact with his fur-covered back, grabbing a loud yelp out of him as her anger burned him at the touch, making him shift right back into human form, reaching down to touch his red side.

"What the fuck?" Ace mumbled under his breath, gaze pinning Lenore.

Shit.

So much for keeping it from him and the others.

This was not going to be good.

That said, neither was her being used as a bargaining chip with the fucking shifters either.

"How the fuck did you get out?" Sully growled at Lenore, though his words weren't as heated as you might think seeing as she'd given him second-degree burns on his side.

"The door locked from the inside, not out," she said, having the balls to roll her eyes at him. "I belong with them," she added, voice gaining some strength.

"You belong here now," Sully objected.

"I'm a person, not a possession," she shot back, even though she was clearly a bit of both to us. They didn't need to know that.

"Afraid you are going to have to be both, witch," Sully said, shrugging. "You're worth too much to just let you go."

"I'd like to see you try to stop me," she challenged, raising her hands at him. I knew what those burns felt like. It was no surprise that Sully flinched when she brushed past him.

"You—" Sully started, only to have the older man put a hand on his shoulder.

"It's not worth it," he said, shaking his head. "We'll find other ways."

"Or other witches," Sully agreed, tone low, lethal, making Lenore shrink back a bit, likely thinking about her coven, and the loved ones she'd left behind there, not wanting to subject them to a similar—or worse—fate than hers. "If any of you step onto our turf again," he said, looking at Ace, "we will consider that a break of the long-standing truce we have known."

"Careful who you threaten," Ace shot back as Lenore moved in at my side, tucking herself a bit behind my shoulder. "Remember what happened the last time you fucked with us," he added, turning on those last words, and getting on his bike.

"Come on," I mumbled to Lenore, grabbing her arm, pulling her over to my bike. "Climb on behind me," I said when she stood there after I got on, unsure what to do. "Legs against the backs of mine, arms around my chest. Then hold on."

Not needing any more instructions, seemingly in as big of a rush to get out of there as I was, she climbed on behind me, and slid forward so I could feel each inch of her against me—her tits on my back a distraction I didn't need when trying to drive us home. Then her arms tentatively slid around my sides, folded across my chest.

"Hold tight," I reminded her as I backed the bike out then flew out of the lot, wanting to put space between her and the shifters as fast as possible.

Her body jolted hard, adjusting to the new sensation. Unless her coven had like... horses and shit... I couldn't imagine she'd ever experienced anything like being on a bike.

After a couple of minutes of clinging to me like she wanted to burrow into my skin, she slowly relaxed, arms releasing just enough to let me breathe properly again.

It was then, too, that her face pressed into my back.

It was nothing.

Or, at least, that was what I needed to believe.

I needed to think of anything other than how nice it felt to have her leaning into me, holding onto me more than she needed to. Almost as if she *wanted* to hold me, to get closer to me.

It was a long drive home.

Too long.

I needed to stop the bike, to grab her, get a taste of her.

I wasn't going to be able to think straight—let alone drive straight—without getting some sort of relief from the growing need inside.

I slowed up, let Minos pass to disappear down a hill, then pulled to the shoulder, reaching for my phone, shooting off a text saying the witch needed a pitstop, and that we were ten minutes behind.

"Why did we stop?" Lenore asked, making no move to pull away from me, arms and legs wrapping me up, cheek on my back.

I didn't answer her.

Not in words, anyway.

I pulled out of her hold, climbing off the bike, grabbing her hips, swiveling her around to face the back of the bike, then pressing her down onto the seat as my hands grabbed at her pajama pants, ripping them down her legs, laying her bare right there in the tree line right off the highway. Not giving a single fuck who happened past, I grabbed her thighs as I leaned down, breathing in her scent for a second before running my tongue up her pussy.

A shuddering gasp escaped her as my tongue found her clit.

A part of me wanted to go easy on her, explore this with her.

The other part was too into it, too beyond needy, overwhelmed with her sweet scent, and sweeter taste. The sounds of her flooded my ears, silencing anything else as her gasps became loud, unabashed whimpers.

Her fingers dug into my hair as my fingers slipped between us, pushing deep into her pussy, thrusting. Hard, fast, unrelenting, driving her up.

She teetered there on the edge for a long moment, her voice crying out, begging for an end to the sweet torment.

My fingers turned inside her, raked over her top wall, as I sucked hard on her clit, making the orgasm slam through her system, calling out my name as she came, her pussy clenching at my fingers as I milked it for all it was worth, licking, sucking, fingers rubbing over her G-spot until her body went languid, spent.

I pulled back, looking down at her pink skin, her heaving chest, her hazy eyes, her wide mouth.

Fuck.

That mouth.

I needed that as much as she needed mine.

More, even.

I reached out, slipped under her neck, grabbing a handful of her long hair, pulling, making her fold, then slip forward, inching off the back of the bike as my hand kept pulling until she was on her feet. My other hand moved out, pressed into her shoulder, pushed her down on her knees.

Her head angled up at me, brows pinched, eyes still a little unfocused, heated, lips still parted.

My finger moved up her neck, my thumb rubbing across her lower lip.

"Suck my cock," I demanded, hearing the raw need in my voice as my hand left her lip, went into my pants, pulled out my aching cock, stroking it down to the base as her eyes widened, recognition hitting.

"Lenore," I growled, snapping her out of her stupor as she looked up at me, then down at my cock, then back up at me.

I grabbed the back of her neck, pulling her forward, feeling the head of my cock press against her lip, then pausing, waiting.

I felt it before I saw it.

The slick, innocent flick of her tongue on the head, lapping up the pre-cum there before her lips spread over me, taking me in.

There was none of the expected awkwardness, the shyness.

Lenore sucked my cock like she was built for it, following the unspoken responses of my body, letting me rock deep, right into the back of her throat, not even trying to pull away as she made little choking sounds as her gag reflex adjusted to the invasion.

"Fuck, yeah, baby, just like that," I growled as she started working me faster, lips sucking tighter.

She didn't stop.

Not even as her eyes watered, as stray tears slipped down her cheeks, as they mingled with the spit and pre-cum from her lips, then dripped down her chin.

"Fuck," I groaned, thrusting harder and deeper, coming so hard that my vision went white for a long second before it cleared again, finding her looking up at me, eyes wide. "Swallow," I demanded as I slowly pulled my cock from her mouth, my hand touching her throat, feeling it as she swallowed back my cum, something that had never seemed quite as hot as it did right then. "Good girl," I said, watching as her lips curved up tentatively, needing the reassurance, reminding me again that this shit was all new to her, and she probably deserved someone who would ease her into it, not fuck the back of her throat like she was any common cut slut I'd come across over the years.

Reaching down, I pulled her back onto her feet, turning her so that her back pressed to my chest, hands going around her, slipping up under her shirt. I cupped her breasts, teasing over the nipples until she was grinding her ass back against me, needy once again, the sweet smell of her practically intoxicating as my hand slid down her stomach, slipped between her legs, slid inside her.

But softer.

Slower.

"Next time, I want my cock here," I told her, lips on her ear, feeling the shudder that moved through her at the idea. "You want that too," I said as my fingers started moving inside her, her greedy walls getting tight already, her hips moving along with my thrusts, her body knowing exactly what it needed even if she wasn't fully initiated in all the ways her body could work with a man yet. "Say it," I demanded as she started to whimper.

"I want it too."

"You want my cock inside your pussy," I insisted, fingers starting to do circles inside her.

"I want... I want your cock inside my pussy," she repeated, voice breathless as her hips rocked harder, faster, wanting nothing of the slow torment, needing release again.

I wasn't done yet, though.

A third finger slipped inside her, widening her, getting those high whimpers to turn into low, throaty moans as she got to feel a hint of what it would feel like to have me inside her, stretching her walls, owning her completely.

Me.

Just me.

It shouldn't have, but the idea of that became important, all-consuming. To be the only one inside her. To claim her as my own.

"And after that," I said, one finger, slick with her wetness, slipped out of her, slid back slightly, pressed, then thrust in, "I want my cock in here," I told her as all three fingers started to thrust in tandem.

Fuck.

The sounds she made as I finger-fucked both her holes, taking every bit of her. She wasn't even touching me, and I swear I was on the edge of coming again just at the noises she was making.

Then just like that, she fucking shattered, crying out so loud the birds in the trees around us startled, flew off as her muscles contracted around my fingers for what felt like ages before they finally released, leaving her body falling back to mine, unable to hold her own weight again.

My arm went around her, holding her to me as my fingers slid out of her.

"Don't ever fucking leave me again," I demanded as she started to even out her breathing.

"I didn't leave you. I was... I just went for a walk. I got lost," she told me, head turning a bit, cheek pressing into my chest. "You came to get me."

"Of course I did."

And, I realized, it didn't have a fucking thing to do with Ace, or the others, or the mission, or anything except my desire to have her close.

"Lycus?" her voice called a moment later, soft, small.

"Yeah?"

"I want you inside me," she told me, voice even lower.

"Greedy pussy," I mumbled, my hand slapping it hard enough to get a shocked whimper out of her. "Not here. Not like this. But you're going to have it," I told her.

A promise.

A vow.

To the two of us.

I was through pretending I had anything even resembling self-control around her.

She wanted it.

I wanted it.

Nothing else mattered.

Except, of course, it did.

But I didn't give that enough thought until it was too late.

Chapter Thirteen

Lenore

The motorcycle was unlike anything I'd ever experienced before.

The second we took off from the shifter clubhouse, it was like my belly bottomed out, like my heart soared out of my chest.

It was terrifying.

And exhilarating.

It was one of the most thrilling moments of my life.

Until, of course, Lycus pulled the bike to a stop on the side of the road, stripped me out of my borrowed pants, and put his mouth on me, that forked tongue of his doing things to me I never could have imagined.

It shouldn't have been as sexy to please as to be pleased, but there was no denying the strange surge of power and joy and pride that flowed through me when I had him in my mouth, when I got those sounds out of him, had been able to bring him to release like he had been able to do with me.

Then.

Well.

His fingers.

And his words.

Even satisfied by him twice, I felt like a puddle of need when we got back to the house, finding all the others already back, gathered around.

"We'll deal with her later," Ace warned as Lycus led me inside. "Put her away for now."

"Put me away," I grumbled.

"Shush," Lycus demanded, grabbing my arm, leading me through to the kitchen, then down the basement stairs. "Don't fuck with Ace when he is pissed off."

"He didn't seem like he was angry."

"Because you don't know him. We're lucky he didn't rip Sully's fucking head off. He would have, for the way he spoke to him. But he wants you more than he wants to spill that shifter's blood. That doesn't mean he won't make you regret running off."

"I didn't run off. I took a walk."

"You knew you were supposed to be locked down here."

"So, I'm at fault for not being a model prisoner?" I shot back, eyes getting small.

"Don't," Ly demanded, sighing.

"Don't what? Tell the truth? Maybe I should have stayed with the shifters. At least they were up-front about what they wanted me for."

To that, Lycus closed his eyes, fighting some internal battle.

"We need your powers," he told me, shrugging.

"I barely have any powers," I objected.

"Tell that to that mutt with his burned side."

"That's... that is different," I told him, not wanting to admit that it was new, that I didn't know I was capable of it until recently. "I don't have much else."

"You have more than the others had. The rain. The burning. It's more. Ace knows how valuable that is. He has a lot of hopes that you can do what the others haven't."

"What's that?" I asked. "What do you want us for? Does it kill us? Is that why you need a new one every generation?"

"It doesn't kill you," he told me. And as forthcoming as he was being suddenly, I could also sense there was a lot he was keeping to himself, that he didn't want me to know.

"Well, something does."

"Yeah, babe, something kills everyone eventually."

"Except you," I said, shaking my head.

"Witches can have immortality if they want it."

"That is dark magic," I objected, feeling a cool sensation wash over me at the very idea.

In my coven, dark magic was talked of in hushed whispers with a lot of head shaking and gasps of disapproval about the methods involved.

"Yes. And even light witches can use dark magic."

"It is selfish," I objected.

"All the best things in life are," he shot back.

"That is a horrible thing to think. Selflessness is—"

"Not something my kind is known for," he cut me off. "Though, I can be generous in some things," he added, giving me a wicked look as his tongue flicked to the side of his mouth, making my sex clench hard at the memory of how it felt on me. "What?" he asked when my gaze fell to the floor. "The fuck is it now?"

"Why do you do that?"

"Do what?"

"Act nice one moment after being cruel right before?"

"Cruelty is my nature, babe."

"And the kindness?"

"Shit. That must be from being up here for so long," he said, shrugging. "The humans rub off on you even if you don't want them to."

"Is it so terrible to be good like them?"

"Oh, babe, come the fuck on," he said, snorting. "Humans aren't good. If they were, the world wouldn't need me or my brothers up there. One human might be good, but as a whole, they're self-absorbed and selfish and petty and nasty. Not even for good reasons, either. Just shitty mortal pride. A need to be right. Don't place humans on a pedestal. They're not better than us."

"You're a *demon*," I shot back, shaking my head at him.

"And I don't act like anything else. I don't lie to get what I want. What you see, is what you get. There is some honor in that. Even if you don't like what I do."

That was, admittedly, fair.

"You act like you care about me," I told him, lifting my chin.

"Fuck," he hissed, turning away from me, inspecting the wall mural for a long moment. "That isn't pretending," he admitted after a meditative moment.

"You are telling me you care about me? As more than a witch for whatever you need my powers for?"

"It makes no fucking sense, but yeah. Yeah. Is that what you want to hear? Something is off here. I feel shit for you that I have no business feeling. Shit I've never felt before. It's fucked up."

"It's... fucked up... to feel something toward me?"

"Toward anyone, babe. I don't catch feelings. I didn't think I was capable. That any of us could be. But here we are. There are feelings. And not just the carnal kind. Though there is that."

"What other feelings?" I pressed, not sure I would ever catch him so candid again, and wanting to understand the situation completely.

"Possessive ones," he admitted, starting with what seemed to be the easiest to admit. Possessiveness was, at its core, a robust, manly trait, an easy feeling to experience, and to admit to having experienced. "You're not mine, but it feels like it. It makes no sense, but that's how it is."

"So you want to... own me?" I pressed, wanting to understand completely.

"Yes. No. Both, I guess," he told me, sighing. "Something inside me looks at you and says, "Mine." And with that comes the need to protect you. Make you happy. I don't fucking understand it, babe. It just is."

"I should hate you," I told him, watching as his head whipped over, gaze penetrating. "That is what I'm supposed to do to a man who took me from my home, my loved ones, who kept me captive, who talked down to me and shamed me and snapped at me even when I did nothing wrong. I should hate you."

"But?" he prompted when I didn't go on. If I wasn't mistaken, there was some vulnerability in his eyes as he asked as well. A demon shouldn't have been capable of it. Vulnerability was a trait of the light, and demons were all dark. Maybe he was right, though. All this time on earth had softened him.

"But I don't. When the shifters found me, and took me back to their home, all I thought about was you," I admitted, the admission making heat creep up the sides of my neck.

"It makes no sense," he said, shaking his head. "Goes against both our natures."

"I know."

"And yet..."

"And yet," I agreed, taking a tentative step closer.

"Can't make you any kind of promises, babe," he told me, closing the distance, his hands sliding around my hips. "I don't have the control here that you'd like me to have."

"None?" I pressed, chin dipping toward my chest, making my forehead brush his chest. "Not even that I will live through this?" I asked. "Whatever this is. Whatever you all want with me."

"Unless shit goes sideways," he started his upper body folding forward, letting his face press into my hair, taking a deep breath, "you are going to live through it."

"Okay," I agreed, nodding.

"Okay? Staying alive—that is all you want?"

"Well, no. I want other things," I said, lips curving up even though he couldn't see my smile.

"Well, those things, I can sure as fuck give you," he told me, voice deep, full of promises. "But not right now," he clarified. "I need to go do some damage control. And you have to stay down here."

"Okay," I agreed, nodding.

"I'll bring you something to eat after I deal with Ace."

"Will I be able to come back to your room again?" I asked, trying not to sound too hopeful.

"Depends."

"On?"

"How sad you will be that you can't be there," he told me, pulling back a bit too smirk down at me.

"Oh, right," I agreed, smile tugging at my lips. "I have a feeling if I am stuck down here for more than a day or two, things might start to get very wet outside."

"Thatta girl," he agreed, fingers moving out to snag my chin, yanking it up, then sealing his lips over mine.

It was meant, I thought, to be an 'until later' kiss, but as soon as our lips met, a fire burned, raged, consumed, until I was clinging to him, and his hands were sinking into my behind, yanking me forward, crushing me against his hardness, making that heat bloom in my core and move outward until it consumed me completely.

My hands slid under his shirt, teased over his hot skin, grazing over the multitude of scars there—raised and smoother than the rest of his skin. I wanted to know their stories, fully aware of the ugliness those tales likely held.

Maybe I wasn't as light as I was supposed to be, as I had been raised to be. I should have rejected everything about the cruelty etched on his skin. Yet there was no denying that I found myself inexplicably fascinated.

The deep sound of a throat clearing was a cold bath raining down on us, making us break apart, turning before we could even draw breaths.

There was Minos, arms folded, cold gaze on Lycus, not even sparing me a glance.

"Shit isn't complicated enough?" he asked, shaking his head. "You know how this is going to go," he added, being deliberately vague about, I imagined, my likely future.

"It's not your business," Ly shot back.

"No," Minos agreed, sighing so deeply, his massive chest look deflated. "But if Ace loses his shit, we are all going to suffer. Maybe especially her. You might want to keep that in mind," he said, turning to go up the stairs, still not looking at me. "Ace wants a meeting. That's why I came down here," he added before disappearing.

"I have to go," Ly told me, taking a deep breath.

"Yes," I agreed, nodding.

"I will get some food down here after," he said, walking toward the stairs, heading up without another word, or even a glance.

Alone, I fell back on the bed, pressing a hand to my beating heart, finding myself confused by the complexity of feelings there. The battle with my old beliefs, and my burgeoning new ones. The resentment and anger I felt toward the demons, with the softness and heat I felt for Lycus.

There had never been any existential crises in my life. I had always known who I was, who my family was, what was expected of me, and how my future would go.

There was nothing to question.

Because there was no other life to live.

Now, though, everything I had known, thought I had wanted, was torn from me, leaving me unsure of who I was, what I might become, or what was expected of me.

I felt a heady mix of fear and uncertainty and excitement and hope.

And, perhaps above all, powerlessness.

But I wasn't powerless.

That thought was like an electric shock to my system, a jolt that buzzed through every nerve ending.

I wasn't powerless.

The demons didn't take me because they wanted to hurt my coven. They didn't seem to take me to hurt me either, to take pleasure in my pain.

No.

Judging by Ly's confirmation that I wouldn't be killed, the fact that no one had hurt me—unless their disregard counted—, the way they had come to take me back from the shifters, and then, of course, the collection of strange research in Ace's room, it all added up to something unexpected.

They needed me.

They needed *me.*

Because of who I was.

Because of what they thought I could do.

A task, I imagined, the other Sacrifices before me had failed.

A task that Lycus appeared to think I could accomplish. That was why he'd wanted me to keep my new power to myself. Because maybe I was the one. Who could give them what they wanted.

I had some sort of power and control in this new world I found myself in.

I just needed to understand what that power was, what they wanted from me, how I could give them that, possibly in exchange for my freedom.

I had no idea what freedom would mean, how I could survive in this new world, but that was all something I would have to figure out.

Once I got free from whatever ties were binding me here.

Free, I wouldn't be so dependent upon these demons. I would have my own agency. I could build my own life.

Did a part of me that I didn't fully understand yet want Lycus to be in that new life?

Yes.

But on my own terms.

Without me feeling like he controlled me.

I had no idea if he would still want me then.
But time would tell.
I just had to wait.
And snoop.
Figure out what Ace was researching.
Then bargain for my freedom.
Come what may.

Chapter Fourteen

Lycus

Of all the people who could have found out about me and Lenore, Minos was likely the best person.

He kept to himself.

If he judged, he did it mostly silently, as he did all things.

He had nothing to say as I walked in the kitchen behind him, grabbing a coffee before joining the others in the study.

Ace had mostly pulled himself back together. His eyes still blazed redder than they typically did on the human realm, but he was more man than beast.

He went on for over an hour about Lenore, about her unexpected power, about how she might be the one, how he might be able to push up the timeline, what everyone's thoughts were on that, if the witch was ready, how we could coerce her into being ready.

He was desperate.

More so than he had been when we'd gotten the newest Sacrifice, likely thinking she would be a disappointment like all of the rest.

But believing there was a chance she was different, that she could handle it, that gave him something truly dangerous.

Hope.

After so many generations of the same old shit, hope was something that could destroy a man like Ace if it was ripped away from him.

"Maybe give her some freedom," Red suggested when we all stayed silent, most of all me, not wanting to draw attention to the fact that I knew more about our current Sacrifice than I should have.

"Why?" Ace asked, needing more data, always the type to compile facts, make sure he had the whole picture.

"Look, I know the method has always been to toss them in the basement, give them the bare essentials, and wait until their spirit is broken enough to use them. But maybe we have been misguided in that. Maybe they are more powerful when they have some control over their own lives. Look what she did back at the shifter clubhouse. Wanting to make a decision, wanting to come back to the devils she knows rather than stay with those glorified dogs, her power surged, right? Maybe that is the key. Maybe if we give them the freedom to move around, to make up their own minds about things, their powers are more stable and strong."

"It's worth a shot," Ace decided, shrugging. "If we can be sure she won't run off."

"Even though she left," Aram said, shrugging, "she willingly came back. I don't think she was trying to leave. She was just craving, like Red said, some freedom. She was raised in the woods, so maybe she wanted to be reconnected to it again."

"Maybe the illusion of freedom," Ace compromised. "She can move around, go into the woods, maybe even go into town, see the world, but not alone. I don't want her sneaking off. Or getting snatched up by anyone else who might sense her power. We will have to guard her."

And that was how I became the personal bodyguard to the witch.

The first few days, everyone took turns. I didn't want to seem too eager to be with her as she was given free rein over her own life, choosing a room on the second floor, going into the woods to collect wild mushrooms and the last fruits on the berry bushes, sometimes just sitting around, staring at nature for hours.

But, as I expected, that guard duty grew old fast for the others who wanted to go back to having the freedom with their own days.

Minos, I suspected, stepped back more so because he knew I wanted to step up. Whether he thought it was a good idea or not.

So step up I did.

Within five days, I had become Lenore's unofficial guard, something we both tried to act indifferent about, if not outright hostile.

I sneered at her.

She snapped at me.

But as soon as we broke into the woods on her nearly daily walks, I was slamming her back against a tree, my lips crashing down on hers.

We explored with hands, with mouths, but things hadn't progressed beyond what we'd already done yet. Partly because of paranoia about being caught, and partly because of my reticence to go there.

I wasn't a soft man.

I didn't do flowers and candy and sweetness.

Yet I found myself wishing they were things I was capable of because some part of me believed she wanted that, she was due that.

I didn't think of sex as special.

It was a function of the bodies.

It was a fun way to spend some time.

But I'd been on this plane, around the humans, long enough to know that first times often were considered something special, something memorable.

I didn't pretend to understand my compulsion to have it be that way for Lenore, but it was there, it was a factor, and so a rushed quickie against a tree limb just didn't exactly feel right.

That said, the need to be inside her was like a flame inside that refused to be extinguished. Each passing day, it got stronger and stronger.

Even as Ace perfected his plans, as he got closer to being sure, being ready to approach Lenore with what would change her life forever.

And I was too chickenshit to tell her, to explain to her what was about to happen, how it might change things, and how it would likely impact what she and I had going.

"Where are we going?" she asked as her foot caught in some underbrush, making her hand shoot out to grab my arm.

She didn't pull it away even when she righted herself.

And I didn't shrug it off either.

There was something right in the feeling of us touching. It was straight out of some sappy fucking romance, but it felt wilder, more primal, like there was something deep within me that responded to her. Not a soul, of course, seeing as I didn't have one. But a softness I didn't know existed, a protectiveness I never would have thought I was capable of.

Mine mine mine that little voice inside me said, only it was getting louder and louder, harder and harder to ignore.

I didn't grasp it on a rational level, but that was what she was.

Mine.

And I wanted her to be mine in every way she could be.

Which was where we were going.

To something I'd gotten up at dawn to prepare.

Something special.

Something memorable.

I knew she was ready.

When it came to putting a stop to things before they went too far, I'd been the one laying on the brakes, having to untangle myself from her as she tried to tell me she was ready, she wanted it, she wanted me.

I didn't realize how much self-control I had until I'd turned her down day after day, night after night when she crept into my room, curled into my body, climbed on top of it, whispering the wicked shit I'd—in recurring bouts of masochism—taught her to say.

Luckily enough, after two or three good orgasms, her mind—along with her body—turned to mush, giving me a chance to rein in my own need to finally be inside her.

It would all be worth it, though, I reminded myself as we followed the trickling creek until I saw our destination.

A massive, ancient Weeping Willow tree, growing close to the water as they often liked to do. Spread beneath was a pile of thick blankets, softening the hard ground, a picnic basket, and a bunch of flowers I'd gathered on my walk in.

"Oh." The breath rushed out of Lenore as she pulled to a stop, taking in the scene, seeming to understand the significance as she turned to me, smile sweet, eyes soft. "Yes, finally," she said, reaching up to grab the sides of my face, drawing me down, pressing her lips to mine.

"You're sure?" I asked, pulling back slightly.

"Absolutely."

Thank fuck.

Chapter Fifteen

Lenore

He'd set a scene.

I'd practically been begging him for days, my ego getting bruised each time he brushed off my desire to have him inside me. I knew he wanted me too, so I couldn't fathom what was making him pull away, push me away, tell me it wasn't right yet.

Because he wanted to set a scene.

He wanted to pick a spot he knew I would like, make it comfortable, get us completely alone so no one could interrupt.

He wanted it to be right.

It was unexpectedly sweet from a man who was not really a man at all, who wasn't, by nature, kind.

He was being kind *for me.*

My heart skittered in my chest at that, a new occurrence I often felt when he was nearby. It was often accompanied by this strange pulling sensation in my chest toward Lycus.

While our coven didn't practice romantic love, we knew of it because we did—during rough times—trade love spells to the human women in town. So we all learned the ways in which it could impact the body, the mind, the soul.

There was a string, an invisible string, that attached soul mates.

The only problem with that scenario was that Lycus, as a demon, had no soul.

So maybe it was in my imagination, this string.

But I felt it.

And it was sweet and reassuring and something I found myself wanting to protect at all costs. Even if our future was uncertain. Even if there were no guarantees that this connection could last.

I guess, in the end, it didn't matter if it did last. All that mattered was that I was given the opportunity to experience it, to delve deeply into it, to take it for all it was worth.

And I was ready to take it, to take him, to move forward with him.

My hands framed his face as I went up on my tiptoes to seal my lips to his, soft and sweet, a thank you for his thoughtfulness, his consideration of my feelings, for wanting to make this something memorable for me.

Ly's hands slid down my back, sinking into my behind, pulling me tightly against him. His hardness pressed into my belly, making the need bloom through my system, something warm and liquid, something I hoped I would never get sick of, never become immune to, this way he could so easily affect me.

He released me to slip his fingers into the waistband of my skirt, pushing it off my hips, letting it drop down onto the forest floor, all but forgotten as his fingertips moved over my skin, creating heat where the cool autumnal air skittered across me.

I never did take to the human custom of underwear, so his palms cupped my bare ass, squeezing, slipping down, sliding between my thighs as his tongue moved inside my mouth to claim mine, getting harder, hungrier, more demanding. More... *him.*

I appreciated him trying to alter his nature for my comfort, but I liked him for who he was. My body responded to his nature with reckless abandon.

His finger traced up my cleft, finding that perfect point of pleasure, moving over it with slow, deliberate circles as his lips crushed, bruised.

"Lycus," I moaned, that deep ache begging for fulfillment.

More.

I needed more.

I needed everything.

Sensing my desperation, likely feeling it himself, his hands moved, his lips ripping from mine so he could pull up my shirt and remove it, toss it to the side with my skirt.

My nipples hardened at the cool air, drawing his attention, his hands moving there, squeezing, grazing, rolling the tightened buds between his thumb and forefinger.

My hungry hands grabbed at his shirt, making him raise it up, allowing me to remove it, tossing it to the side. My fingertips traced over his heated skin, seeing the muscles tense under the inspection. As my fingers teased over the lowest part of his stomach, a hiss escaped him.

I undid his button and zipper, drawing his pants down over his hips, finding his cock already thick and straining, making my walls tighten in anticipation.

My gaze lifted to his as I slowly lowered myself down to the ground, taking him into my mouth.

His hands went to my head, holding on as I worked him the way I knew he liked best—fast, deep, unrelenting, messy. The longer I sucked him, the more I could feel his talons digging into my scalp. The more desperate he got for release, the more the Change would come upon him. The talons. The forked tongue. The more pointed teeth that had once bitten hard enough into my inner thigh to leave bloody imprints for two days. The horns would protrude ever so slightly in the moments right before he came, but I had yet to see him lose control completely, have those dark wings he'd mentioned emerge.

His fingers grabbed my hair, yanking roughly back until his cock slid from my mouth with a pop.

His thumb moved across my swollen lower lip, his gaze heated, but unreadable for a long moment before he lowered down to his knees as well, pressing me back against the soft blankets.

Ly planted his hands on the blanket, his lips moving down my neck, over my breasts, licking, then sucking my nipple into his mouth until I arched up into him, a moan escaping me.

Releasing me, he started a trail downward, his tongue tracing down the center of my belly, the crease of my thigh, then inward, licking up my cleft, moving over my clit with expert precision, driving me up hard and fast, pushing me over the edge before I could even tell I was teetering there.

The orgasm surged through me, but he gave me no time to come back down, his tongue moving away from my clit for a moment, but still licking, teasing, as his fingers moved between us, surged inside. Soft and slow at first, but building in intensity, his fingers spreading with each thrust, preparing me, widening me. A third finger slipped inside, a small pinch accompanying the invasion, but quickly forgotten as the new, fuller sensation created an intensity that felt almost overwhelming.

His tongue moved back to my clit as he thrust—harder, faster, deeper—driving me back up to that edge.

But as soon as he had me there, his tongue left me, his fingers slid out.

He straightened, sitting back on his calves, looking down at me with eyes that were nearly fully red with desire as he grabbed his cock, coating it with my wetness from his fingers before dragging my hips toward him slightly.

I could feel my belly wobble as my walls fluttered, knowing this was it. The wait was over. We were both beyond anything even resembling resistance.

He leaned forward, his cock pressing against my opening, feeling suddenly even bigger, thicker, than I'd realized. It pressed there before pushing a little harder, creating an unexpected burning sensation that had my breath gasping inward.

Ly's gaze slid to mine, wild, but worried.

"No?" he asked, voice tight.

"I...yes," I said, already feeling the burning sensation easing. "You're just... big," I told him, taking a deep, steadying breath.

"I can't make it not hurt," he told me, tone apologetic.

"It's okay," I told him, my hand moving down, grabbing his. "You'll make it better."

He gave me a tight nod at that as his hips shifted forward again, giving me more of the burn as my body adjusted to the invasion.

When he had inched halfway in, he started to rock in his already charted territory, creating that friction my body told me it needed. His free hand moved toward my clit again for a long moment, driving me up.

But then his hands sank into my hips, yanking them toward himself as he slammed forward, taking every inch of me, the pain immediate, making me cry out even as his body curled over mine, lips claiming mine.

"Just give it a minute," he begged against my lips before kissing me. Soft, sweet, deep, distracting me from the pain.

It wasn't long before I could feel that tight ache inside, that deep pressure, having my hips tentatively rocking against him, testing out the sensation, seeing if there was more of that same pain. It was there, at first, but less intense, melting away as my body got hotter, got needier.

"Ly, please," I whimpered, hands going around him, hips moving in small circles.

His head lifted, red eyes on me, reading my face. "Yeah?" he asked, voice a growl.

My walls tightened around him, making him curse.

"Yes," I agreed, nearly mindless with the need for release, somehow knowing it would feel different like this, with him creating this delicious fullness.

He was slow at first, careful, sweet, barely rocking inside me, even as his body seemed to get tighter, more desperate for release.

"I have to," he told me, confusing me for a second before I felt him starting to thrust harder, faster.

"Yes," I whimpered into his ear, fingernails digging into his back as my feet planted, allowing me to move in circles as he kept thrusting.

He balanced his weight on one hand, reaching back to grab my wrist, drawing my hand between our bodies, pressing my fingertips against my clit, giving me the motion, then releasing me, planting again, as I started to work myself.

Ly pushed up slightly, looking down at me with eyes that seemed to dance with flames as he fucked me harder, faster, nearly leaving me completely each time before slamming deep, his voice coming out like animalistic growls, sounds that mingled with my uncontrolled moans and whimpers as my surged higher once more, as I started to tighten around him.

"Fuck. Come, Lenore," he demanded, his body rigid, begging for release. "Come," he demanded again as he thrust forward while my finger instinctively pressed down, creating a pressure that made the orgasm soar through me, my walls contracting around his thickness, creating that sensation I knew would come, but couldn't have known how overwhelming it would feel as the waves kept crashing through me, around him.

On the tail-end of my orgasm, he slammed forward, harder than before, deeper, claiming every bit of me as he let out a growl as his body jolted.

As he came, those wings I had been wondering about burst out from his flesh, spreading wide behind him.

Darkly beautiful.

Magnificent.

"Fuck," he hissed, his weight crashing down on me, crushing me, as he gasped for breath, trying to get some control back over his body. His heartbeat pounded in rhythm with mine, his too-hot body feverish, warming me even as the sweat dried, cooling me.

After a long moment, he shifted slightly, rolling me onto my side against him, his wings closing around me like an embrace, cocooning me in his warmth, tickling over my skin for a moment before they settled.

I had never felt warmer, safer, or more protected from the world.

Or happier.

God, the happiness felt like I had swallowed the sun, like it was bursting out of my fingertips.

There was soreness too—a tenderness between my thighs, an ache in my thigh muscles, but they only seemed to add to the moment as this man's arms held me tight, as his lips pressed into the top of my head.

"I want your wings like this always," I told him, lips brushing his chest as I spoke.

"Good," he agreed, voice still rough. "Because I can't seem to force them back," he admitted.

"Is that normal?"

"No," he said with a snort. "It's not good either. I can't exactly walk around the human world with demonic wings out."

"It'll be okay," I assured him, my fingers trailing over some of his scars, memorizing them. "Wait..." I said, pulling back slightly to look up at his face. No horns, like I suspected. "Your fingers are normal," I observed, feeling them tease up and down my spine. "And your horns went back in. Let me see your tongue," I demanded, getting a small chuckle out of him before he stuck it out at me, letting me see the fork had disappeared. "I don't understand," I admitted. If the talons, horns, and tongue were normal again, and his body heat went back from hellfire to a mild fever, it didn't make sense that his wings were still out in all their glory.

"I don't either," he admitted, shrugging. "Even when I get the Change, the wings are the last to come out," he explained. "It might just take longer for them to go back."

"Well, good," I decided, reaching out tentatively. "May I?" I asked, pausing before touching them.

"You can touch me anywhere you want, babe," he told me, making my belly wobble.

"Does it hurt?" I asked when my fingers brushed his wing, finding it unlike a bird's, but more like a bat's—smooth, velvety. He'd flinched at the contact, his brows drawing together.

"No," he said, shaking his head.

"You're sure?" I pressed. "You're flinching," I told him as my fingers drifted over the wing, unable to get enough of the feel of them.

"It's nothing. It feels... good," he admitted, sounding confused.

"Does it not normally feel good?" I asked, flattening my hand against the softness.

"It usually burns. Me and whoever touches them."

"Really?" I asked, watching his face, looking for any dishonesty, but I found none. If anything, I saw the confusion that I felt as well as some sort of vulnerability that he seemed to save for me.

"Yeah."

"Does this... I don't know... mean something?" I asked.

"Fuck if I know," he admitted, taking a breath so deep it shook his chest.

"We'll figure it out," I told him, tracing over the thick ligament-like webbing that held his wings out.

"Yeah," he agreed, his hands moving over me again like he couldn't get enough of touching me. I understood that feeling well. "You alright?"

"Amazing," I countered.

"I hurt you."

"You made it better," I told him, like I knew he would.

"It'll get better."

"I don't know if that is possible," I told him, getting a seeing look flood his eyes as his lips twitched.

"Sounds like a challenge to me."

"I mean... I wouldn't object to being a part of that."

"Good. Because I am going to fuck you up and down that house every chance I get," he told me, making a little shiver of anticipation move through me.

"Sounds like a great way to spend the rest of my life," I agreed. "Thank you for this," I told him. "This was nice of you. With the blankets and the creek. It's lovely. Reminds me of home."

"Are you hungry?" he asked, making me realize I'd completely forgotten about the picnic basket.

"Yes."

So then we sat up, me wincing just a bit at the tenderness I felt, but he seemed to sense it without even looking at me, his wings moving out to stroke over my back almost like fingertips, comforting me.

Ly turned me and pulled me back against his chest, both of us facing the creek as we picked at the food selection.

I giggled when his wings went around me again.

"That's kind of possessive," I decided.

"Babe, I'm not doing that," he told me.

"What do you mean you're not doing it? They're attached to you. That would be like saying your fingers aren't touching my breast right now," I told him as his thumb moved up and down around the side of my breast.

He let out a small chuckle at that, his hand sliding out to squeeze the swell hard before moving down to anchor across my stomach instead.

"I don't know. I don't fucking get it either. But I am not telling my wings to keep touching you or going around you. They are just doing it."

"Do you have any like... demon texts or anything?" I asked. "To reference."

"If demon texts exist, I doubt they do on the human plane."

"We can look."

"Sure," he agreed.

"It would be good to know more about it. Especially if it keeps happening."

As the minutes passed to a few hours, his wings eventually retreated, leaving me naked and cold, despite having him behind me, body always cozy warm.

"We should head back," he murmured against my hair.

I took a deep breath, closing my eyes, taking one more moment to memorize everything about this. "Okay," I agreed, untangling from him, taking the clothes as he passed them to me.

"Leave it," he demanded when I bent to grab the basket. "I will come back for all of this later. "Let's go get you a bath," he added, tempting me with something he knew would make me happy to get back to the house.

His arm went around my shoulders, hauling me into his side, which made walking awkward, but I didn't want to pull away.

We both did so, though, instinctively, a few yards before the edge of the tree line, knowing we couldn't be caught.

Making our way in the house, we intended to walk past the group in the living room to go up the stairs for my bath, but Ace called to Ly, making us both deflate a bit as we turned.

"You," Ace said, pointing toward me.

It wasn't an overly aggressive gesture.

But something in Lycus responded to it, his wings bursting outward, one wrapping around me, pulling me closer to his body.

"Oh, for fuck's sake," Ace said, eyes widening, lips parting. "You can't be fucking serious, Ly," he added.

"What the hell is going on?" Drex asked, swirling his whiskey, but his body had gone tense.

"You fucking idiot," Ace raged, gaze on Ly, tone accusing.

"Ace, babe," Red said, perfectly arched brow raising, "you gonna let us in one what is going on?"

"This fucking idiot Claimed the witch."

"Claimed," Red repeated, brows furrowing, seeming to have no idea what that meant.

My gaze moved around the room, seeing confused looks on all the other's faces, uncertainty in everyone except Ace—and as the eldest demon, that made sense—and, of all people Minos. And if I wasn't mistaken, there seemed to be pain in his eyes as well. Almost as if he knew what Claiming was, and had experienced it. And possibly lost it.

"Yes, Claimed, Red," Ace said. "Am I the only one who paid attention to our history?"

"Apparently," Aram agreed. "The fuck is Ly going all batty for?"

"He fucked the witch," Seven guessed.

"It's more than that," Ace said, shaking his head. "They're bonded now. Even in human form, the demon part of him will protect her at all costs. Right down to his own life."

"Oh, fuck," Drex said, sighing.

"Yeah," Ace agreed.

"How will we use the witch now?" Drex asked.

"Exactly," Ace agreed.

Beside me, nestled close because his wing insisted upon it, Lycus was stony silent. And just... stony. His whole body was rigid.

I couldn't tell how he was feeling about this whole situation. Was he a willing participant, in a cognitive, aware way, or was this some primal instinct he had no choice but to follow through with?

Did he want this?

Did he want *me*?

An undeniable ache started across my chest, spread upward, closing around my throat, snaking up the backs of my eyes where tears formed.

Around me, his wing tightened, as if sensing my turmoil, responding to it, wanting to ease it. And as sweet as that was, I wanted to know if he *wanted* that.

"Witch," Ace started.

"Lenore," Lycus corrected, tone rough.

"Fine," Ace sighed. "Lenore. Why don't you go up and take a bath?" he suggested. "I can smell Ly all over you," he added. "Ly and the rest of us need to have a talk."

"Ly?" I whispered, worried. About him. About what might happen if he was alone with them.

"It's okay," he said, taking a deep breath. "Go take your bath. I will come up in a bit," he assured me, his wing dropping, allowing me to move away.

I kept my gaze on the gathered demons as I made my way up the stairs.

Well, all but Ly.

Who wasn't looking at me.

My stomach tensed, but I made myself keep walking.

Up the stairs, into his room, into the bathroom where I drew the water, put in some lavender-scented soap Ly had brought me, then stripped and climbed in.

I went ahead and stressed from there, listening to raised, angry voices, wondering what was being said, what was being done, how Ly and I would fare through this new development.

I had just finished re-running the water when I heard footsteps on the stairs, down the hall, through the bedroom.

I opened my eyes to find Ly standing there in the doorway, looking ragged, tired.

Seeing me, his nostrils flared slightly, his eyes going redder, his wings moving out.

"We need to talk."

"About?" I asked, feeling my belly tense.

"About what happens next."

Chapter Sixteen

Lycus

Ace spewed facts at the lot of us for the next twenty minutes, things that we must have learned at some point, but when life was immortal, things got shaken from the brain, replaced with more pertinent information.

Demons were capable of Claiming a mate.

It wasn't something that happened often. In fact, Ace—who had been around for much longer than any of us—had only heard of it happening a handful of times.

His gaze had slid to Minos while he spoke. And Minos's gaze was downcast, guarded.

"I think it happens here more often," Ace mused. "Back home, we are busier. We have missions. There isn't time. But when we come up here, when we are stuck here as long as we have been stuck here, when the mind gets idle, and defenses get low, that is how it can happen."

"And when it happens?"

"When it happens, it happens. There is no undoing it."

"Except?" I asked, jerking my chin toward Minos, suddenly understanding his withdrawn, miserable nature, why he so infrequently came out anymore, why he always seemed to be hurting over something.

How had I missed him Claiming someone?

And who had it been?

Where was she now?

"Except if she rejects you," Ace said. "You still Claim them. If you are near them, your nature responds, you protect them. But if she rejects you, it creates a deep cavern inside that never gets filled again."

Shit.

I felt like a terrible friend to Minos suddenly.

"It doesn't seem like she is rejecting him," Aram said.

"She looks up at him with puppy-dog eyes," Red agreed.

"The question comes back to how we use the witch if Ly here goes all homicidal if anyone even looks at the witch—*Lenore,*" Drex said when a rumble moved through me, my talons poking out from my fingertips.

Ace sighed, raking a hand through his hair.

"I guess we ask her to do it," Ace mused.

"Ask her? You'd think she'd be willing to do that?" Red asked, scoffing.

"I think she might. If she knows what I can offer her," Ace said, eyes bright.

About an hour later, I was making my way up the stairs, feeling older than I had when I'd walked into the house, body tired, mind conflicted.

But I had to bring the facts to her.

I had to give her the choice.

It wasn't mine to make.

I told her we needed to talk.

About what came next.

"Okay," Lenore agreed, taking the towel I handed to her even as damn near every nerve ending wanted me to toss her up on the counter and fuck her until everything else slipped away.

I didn't for two reasons.

One, she was still sore.

Two, this was important.

There would be time for fucking later. Depending on what her decision was.

"Are you okay?" she asked, eyes concerned, gaze roaming over me like she might find injuries.

"Fine. But we need to talk about what comes next."

"Okay," she agreed, grabbing one of my tees, slipping it on. "What comes next?"

"You have some decisions to make," I told her, kicking off my shoes, climbing onto the bed, patting the spot beside me.

Lenore, emboldened by our time together, didn't move next to me. No, she climbed onto my lap, straddling me instead.

"What decisions do I have to make?"

"If you are going to willingly help us."

"Okay. Help you do what?"she asked, eager to know what generations of her witch sisters were used for.

"Open a hell mouth."

"A hell mouth?" she repeated.

"A hole between the human plane and hell."

"That's what you want us for," Lenore said, lips parting. "You think we have the power to open a hell mouth."

"You *do* have the power to open a hell mouth. Witches are the only beings capable of doing so," I told her. "We just haven't found a powerful enough witch."

"What happens to the witches?" she asked, tone grave.

I took a deep breath, knowing this was a blow she didn't want to take. "In the past? The ritual drained every bit of power from their bodies. Everything. Even the ability to interpret their cards or runes was gone. They become completely mortal."

It took a long moment for her the words to truly penetrate, leaving her looking stricken. "You took away everything?"

"Yes." There was no use softening the blow. The truth was the truth.

"What happened to them then?"

"They were useless to us," I told her, shrugging. "Ace gave them books, money, set them free."

"Free in a world they didn't understand with no loved ones, no way to go back home?" she asked, eyes tearing up.

My wings moved out, circling around her. "Yes."

"That's cruel."

"Yes," I agreed. "We are, by nature, cruel, Lenore."

"Have any of you checked on them?"

"No, why would we?"

Her gaze slid from mine at that, her head shaking. "Why only one of us?" she asked. "Each generation, why only one? If you drain us?"

"Because it takes a long-ass time to find potential sites for hell mouths. That is what Ace is obsessed with, finding them."

"That's what the map was about," she said, making my brows draw together.

"What map, babe?"

"The map. In his room. I found it the day you all left. That was why I was in the woods. I was trying to figure out what was in the woods that he wanted, thinking it might be the key to what you all wanted from me. I was right. He thinks he found another site."

"Yes."

"And he needs me to try to open it. Even if it drains me."

"Yes."

"I'm not sure what choice I have now."

"Claiming you means they can't make you do anything without me fighting to the bitter end," I told her, my hands sliding up and down the sides of her thighs.

"And they are loyal to you."

"Exactly," I agreed, glad she was being rational about all this. No waterworks, no screaming.

"Okay. So what is my choice?"

"Ace knows a ritual."

"For me?"

"Yes, for you. He says he can make you immortal."

"Immortal. That's not possible," she objected. "I mean, mostly. We can elongate our lives. With certain spells. The elder members of the coven do it while they wait for someone else to become strong enough to step into their positions. But it doesn't last. Lasting immortality is..."

"Evil," I filled in for her, waiting for her to put the pieces together.

"You want me to become evil?"

"You would never become fully evil," I told her. "You would simply have some evil in you. You've already had some evil inside you," I added, lips curving up.

"Oh," she said, eyes going wide, lips parting, likely thinking of all the repercussions that came along with what we had done.

"You're not."

"Not what?"

"Pregnant."

"Demons can reproduce."

"Yes," I agreed. "But when we choose to."

"Okay," she said, taking a deep breath. "So, what happens? If I make that choice?"

"I give you some of my blood. You do the ritual. You become immortal."

"Does this happen before or after the other ritual?"

"After. No one knows if the ritual will strip you of your powers too. So we need that done first."

"But... but if I open the hell mouth, you will all go back to hell."

She didn't say it, but I heard it nonetheless.

You will leave me.

"No. According to Ace, I won't be able to go back."

"Because you Claimed me?"

"Yes. I will stay with you. Minos won't be able to go back either. We have to stay."

"Have to," she repeated.

"What?" I asked, something inside me responding to something in her, something sad.

"I have a question about this Claiming."

My stomach clenched, wondering if this was it, if she was rejecting me, if I would be cursed to a life of misery like Minos.

"Okay."

"Do you want it?"

"Do I want what?"

"Do you want to Claim me? Was that a choice? Or did it happen to you? Are you mad about it? Would you prefer it if it never happened?"

Oh, so that was it.

She was feeling insecure, unsure.

"I couldn't have Claimed you if I didn't want to," I told her. "I don't pretend to know the process, but I know it only happens if the desire for it is there."

Mine mine mine.

That was what that little voice had been saying in my head for a while now.

That was the Claiming beginning to make itself known.

Having sex with her had sealed it, making her mine in every way.

Mine mine mine.

For all of eternity.

If she took the deal.

"So you want me? And this?"

"Babe, I think we both know I want you," I told her, hands sinking into her hips, dragging her higher on my lap where my cock was already straining for her, like it always was when she was near.

Her breath caught, her eyes going heavy, but she shook her head. "That's not what I meant," she told me.

"I want you, babe. In every way. I can't change it. But, what's more, I don't *want* to change it."

"Stop," she demanded, breath starting to get fast.

"Stop what?"

"Looking at me like that."

She was already getting wet for me, that sweet smell flooding my nostrils.

"Can't help it. Lenore, no," I said when she wiggled against me, riding my cock through my pants. "Too soon."

"I need you. We have to. I can't think straight until I have you," she told me, whimpering a little when her clit moved over my cock.

I couldn't claim being noble came easily to me. And I only had a small amount of self-control with regard to her.

I knew it was probably too soon.

But with her looking at me like that, rocking against me like that, I couldn't deny her what she wanted as her hands moved between us, freeing my cock.

"No, like this," I demanded when she went to move off my body.

"Like this?" she repeated, brows furrowing.

"Lift up a little," I told her, waiting for her to do so, then grabbing my cock, sliding it up her wet pussy, getting it good and wet before I pushed it against the entrance to her body. "Now slide down," I demanded.

She did so.

A little too fast, not taking heed of her aching walls, letting out a cry as my cock filled her completely.

"Ouch," she said, taking a deep breath.

"Just ride me, babe," I demanded, rocking my hips. "Ride me, and it will feel all better."

Her hands went to my shoulders as she started to wiggle her hips. She started in slow circles, testing the sensations, then back and forth, then sliding up and down my length.

"Oh," she whimpered.

My legs cocked up behind her. "Lean back a little," I demanded, and she didn't hesitate to do so.

"*Ohhh*," she moaned when my cock started to press against her G-spot.

"Yeah," I agreed, moving my hips in circles as she rode me, one of my hands going between her thighs, working her clit as her walls started to tighten around me.

"I love having you inside me," she admitted, voice a small whisper.

"You're going to love it even more in a minute," I told her as she kept getting tighter and tighter, close to the edge. "Come," I demanded, tapping her clit for a second before pressing hard, feeling her whole body jolt as her orgasm slammed through her system, leaving her screaming out my name.

Her walls kept clenching around me, milking my orgasm from me. And nothing in my long, everlasting life had ever felt as good as coming with her, knowing she would have me inside her, even after my cock slid out.

"Can you think better now?" I asked later, my cock still inside her because she refused to let me move. She'd folded forward into my chest, my wings going around her, holding her close.

"Mmm. Okay."

"Okay?" I repeated.

"Yes. I will do it. I need a lifetime of this. Many lifetimes of this," she added, sighing into me.

I felt hope swell up inside.

But I didn't take her at her post-orgasm word right then.

But when her mind was the same the next day after sleep and food, then I went to Ace with her answer.

And we set the plan in motion.

Chapter Seventeen

Lenore

I wasn't sure what was the appropriate weather for a day that would change your life forever, but mostly cloudy with the occasional burst of hopeful sun seemed rather appropriate. And that was what we got.

We'd all gotten up before dawn, dressing, having breakfast, then meeting in the study where Ace—in an act of good faith—handed me the written ritual along with the items I would need, including a small vial of Ly's blood.

My eyes roamed over it, committing the words to memory the way I had been trained to, even though I would never need this one again.

There was no way to reverse the ritual, either.

For better or for worse, if I did it, I would be immortal. A small part of me would be evil. It could change me.

Then again, so much of me had changed already.

It had been just over a week since Ly and I first became intimate. As he had promised, it had only gotten better each time, the pain slipping away, replaced with only pleasure.

And with the Claiming, we had grown closer in every possible way, staying up late to talk, sharing stories, secrets, hopes for our very long future together.

I was a softer, yet harder, woman at the same time.

Loving a man like Lycus could do that to you.

Yes, love.

I had known it since the string sensation realization. It had only grown since then. With each shared kiss, touch, every whispered admission, every shared fear, every motion and sigh as we moved together.

It wasn't anything like I would have thought, being in love.

It was better.

Good enough that I was willing to lose my powers, to commit to evil, to promise him an unending forever.

There were sacrifices, ones my former self would never have seen myself agreeing to. But this newer version of me didn't even see them as sacrifices.

Had it not been for Ly, for his Claiming me, I would have been forced into giving up my powers. At least, this way, I had a choice. I got something in return.

"Thank you," I said, nodding.

"Let's find the hell mouth," he said in response, still not happy about the situation. Because, as Ly had told me, he had a lot of hope about the strength of my powers. And he didn't like the idea of working so long and so hard at this to lose one of his men forever.

Two, technically.

Poor Minos.

But Ace would get to go home, where he had been trying to go for generations. That kind of homesick was unimaginable. I missed my home. I missed my mother, especially. But as the time stretched on, for me, the homesickness became duller, not stronger as it seemed to for them.

With that, we all made a line out the back of the house, Ly moving in beside me, his wing curling around me, locking in his body heat when I shivered.

I was sure I would never get sick of the way he responded to me without any thought at all. If I was cold or scared or even just wanted affection, his wings were around me, protecting me, blanketing me in his love, locking the rest of the world out.

"I picked the wrong shoes for this," Red declared, grumbling, as the walk stretched on for hours.

Demons might not die, but they felt pain. And I didn't envy Red the blisters likely forming on her feet. But she'd claimed she wanted to look her best for her homecoming. Ly told me because she'd left a demon she cared about behind.

"Not too much longer," Ace assured everyone and their falling spirits. "It's just past that rock formation," he said, pointing.

Then, just like that, we were there, gathered in a semi-circle.

"You were right," I told Ace, stepping out from Ly's hold, hand extended, feeling the tingling sensation on my palm—an undeniable sizzle of power at this point. I knew it from our sacred ritual space deep in the woods. That was where we went to do spells that needed more power than we individually, or collectively, possessed.

"Here," Ace said, holding out another sheet of paper with old, curved handwriting.

The spell for opening the hell mouth.

"Get it done," he added, voice rough as I stepped forward, feeling Lycus's wing caress across the back of my neck before I moved out of reach.

My stomach was tight and swirling as the first words started coming out of my mouth.

I could feel the spell moving through me, conjuring up my magic—what little I had of it—and pulling it toward my fingertips.

"Keep going," Ace told me, voice reassuring, as mine faltered, feeling the ground vibrate beneath me. "Louder now," he demanded on my fifth read-through of the spell, my mouth getting dry. "Louder, witch," Ace shouted.

"*Shut up!*" I shouted, frustrated with my seeming lack of progress.

And just like that, the vibrating became more like an earthquake.

Before I could even think to move, Ly's arms were reaching out, yanking me backward as the floor became much like lava, hot, melting the forest floor inward as the earth opened up.

"Holy shit," Drex hissed.

"This is it," Ace said, gaze going to me, eyes wide. "This is it," he said again, tone disbelieving, before his gaze slid back to the hell mouth that was steadily opening.

"I don't know what you idiots are waiting for," Red said, shaking her head. "I have a hot date with an unrepentant sinner," she added, smiling wide as she jumped forward into the hole.

"Wait—" Ace tried, but it was too late, she was gone.

"Ace," Drex said, clamping a hand on his shoulder. "This was your baby. You go ahead," he said, nodding.

Ace cast his gaze around the group, eyes warm, excited, hopeful, pleased. He was ready to go home.

"Lenore," he said, giving me a nod. "Thank you," he told me. "For your sacrifice. I hope you and Ly have a nice life together. Minos," he called, turning to his other man. "May you know some peace," he said to his old friend. "It's been an honor knowing you."

With that, he moved to take a step forward.

But before he could drop down in the hole like Red had done, to go home after so long, there was a strange rippling of the ground, a high-pitched shrieking sound.

"Lenore?" Ace asked, looking over at me.

"I'm not doing that," I assured him. "What's going on?"

"I have no fucking idea," Ace said.

"Whatever it is, I don't think we should jump into the flaming hole just yet," Aram decided, staring at it as it continued to shriek.

"Yeah, I don't intend—" Ace started, voice drowned out by the screaming as it got loud enough to cause a headache to pierce through my skull.

Then there was a loud pop, making all our bodies duck instinctively.

And there they were.

Two men.

Two *demons*.

In place of the now-closed hell mouth.

"Fuck!" Ace raged, raking a hand through his hair.

"Who the fuck are you?" Drex asked, looking down at the two new demons.

"Hey, look, Earth," one of them declared.

Tall and somewhat thin, he had a wickedly handsome face full of sharp lines, bright green eyes with flecks of red, a scar down his left cheek, other scars covering his hands, and a head of black hair.

"Well," he added, jumping up, brushing off his clothes. "Where are all these women I hear about up here? The ones who can, and I quote, 'suck the paint off a car.' I'm not entirely sure what that means, but I am happy to find out," he added, casting a devilish smile around those gathered. "Oh, hey, here's one. Does she suck—" he started before Ly's wings burst outward again, grabbing me, pulling me close. "Alrighty. Message received."

"Who the fuck are you?" Ace asked, stepping forward slightly.

"Oh, me? I'm Daemon."

"Daemon, the demon," I repeated, feeling a nervous laugh bubble up and burst out.

Daemon shot me that wicked little smile of his as he reached down, offering his hand to his comrade. "And this here is Bael," he said as the other demon gained his feet.

Much like Daemon, Bael was tall. But that was where the similarities ended.

Bael was square-jawed with dark, deep green eyes, with their signature red flecks. He was built more solidly, strongly. And his hair was the deepest shade of red possible before it looked black.

There were no smiles from this demon.

Everything about him seemed serious, angry.

"And he doesn't want to be here," Daemon said, shrugging.

"Then why is he?" Ace asked.

"Because my stupid fucking brother thought it would be smart to hijack a hell mouth to the human plane," Bael said, voice rough. "I tried to stop him. Only to get pulled up here too. How did you open a hell mouth?" he asked.

Aram's gaze slid to me, making Bael's follow.

"A witch," he snapped, eyes turning to dancing flames. "You know, the only witch I've had the pleasure of knowing was one sent to me for betraying her coven during the Trials. Oh, how she screams," he added, lips curving up into the most evil smile I'd ever seen, making my stomach twist.

"Watch it," Ly demanded, body Changing.

I remember Lycus telling me that when they first came to the human plane, they had very little control over the Change.

As Bael's Change came over him in a blink, I guess it proved him right.

"Enough," Ace growled, voice taking on a tone I hadn't heard before, one that seemed to echo, like it was hollow, making Bael's change disappear as quickly as it had appeared.

"You're their leader?" Bael asked, looking at Ace.

"And seeing as I pull rank, it looks like I am your leader now, too."

"I don't want to be here," Bael insisted.

"Join the fucking club," Ace said, turning to walk away, looking at Seven as he waved toward the new demons. "They're on you. I don't have the patience to raise more puppies."

"Ace," Ly called, making him turn back. Lycus waved to me.

"Yeah," Ace agreed, nodding. "A deal is a deal."

With that, he was gone.

"So... women? Sucking?" Daemon asked, practically bouncing with excitement. "Oh, give a man a break. It's been all doom and gloom and shoving hot pokers into people for the last couple hundred years. I need a vacation," he said when everyone stood there staring at him, not sure what to make of him.

"We need to fill you in on how Earth is now," Seven reasoned.

"Yeah yeah, boring school shit," Daemon agreed. "I get it. What's with the cute little matching uniforms?" he asked, gesturing toward the demons' MC cuts. "Hey, Bael, do you want a little matching uniform too? I rather like it."

"Shut the fuck up," Bael responded, seething.

"He's always like this," Daemon said, shaking his head.

"Yes, Daemon. When you trap us on the human plane for all of motherfucking eternity, I do get like this."

"He is desperately in need of the aforementioned sucking as well. Clearly," he added with a smirk, getting a rough smack to the back of the head from his brother.

"Okay," Seven said, patience wearing thin. "Let's all get back to the house. We can talk about shit there," he went on. "Ly, Lenore... when you're done, I think Ace expects you back as well."

The original plan was our freedom, since all the others save for Minos would be gone.

But with the new developments, I understood the change to the plan.

With that, they all trudged off, leaving us alone in the woods.

"We can wait," I said, still feeling a tingle of power inside me, perhaps weaker than before, but still there, still usable.

"We had a deal," Ly insisted.

"But the other witches..." I said, thinking of my coven.

"You won't even know the next one. It will be years before we find another hell mouth. And, besides, if you are around, you can oversee her treatment," he suggested, eyes understanding. "If we don't do the spell, you won't be here for that," he added.

That was true.

Taking a deep breath, I handed Ly the paper to hold out for me to read as I arranged the supplies Ace had given me.

"It's all ready," I declared a few moments later.

"It's going to be okay," Lycus assured me, even though we both knew he couldn't make me that promise. "Or you can wait," he added, and I swear his wings slumped at the very suggestion.

"No. No. I don't want to wait. I'm sure about this," I told him, feeling that string in my chest pull tighter. "I've never been so sure of anything before."

With that, I took a deep breath, lit the bundle of herbs, and started the chant, feeling the magic left in me stir. But this time, it didn't go toward my hands. No, it went to some place just below my ribcage.

The chant was repeated four times, making the magic sing stronger inside me, and a chill move over my skin, like the good part in me was fighting against the heat I was inviting inside, the hellfire that went against my nature.

With my free hand, I flicked off the top of the vial of Lycus's blood, my gaze finding his.

"Forever," he told me, pulling that string tighter still.

I gave him a nod, unable to speak outside of the spell, lifted the vial, and emptied it into my mouth before my stomach and taste buds could roil with the idea of drinking his blood.

This time, when the chant came from me for the final time, my voice was louder, stronger, almost foreign to my own ears.

The blood moved downward, seeking the magic, finding it, mingling together, then flowing through me.

"This is it," I told him, done with the chant. "Forever," I added as the heat moved through me, spreading outward until it burned through every bone, organ, tissue, into my bloodstream, until it hummed and screamed into my now half-blackened soul.

"Do you feel it?" Ly asked, moving closer, his wings lifting upward again, reaching out, stroking over my cheek. "Because I can feel it. You're warm."

"I feel it," I agreed, nodding.

A part of me had been afraid I would feel wicked, that I would suddenly want to maim and torture, and that there would be ugly thoughts inside me.

So far, though, I didn't sense any of that.

"There's something else, though," I told him, feeling it tingling within.

"What's that?"

"I don't think it's gone."

"What isn't?"

"My magic. I don't think it's gone. I actually think... I mean I can't be certain..."

"You think what, babe?"

"I think it might be stronger."

"Yeah?" he asked, eyes burning a little red.

"Yeah. That means I might be able to open up another hell mouth. For them in the future. So they can go home. And they wouldn't need to take another Sacrifice."

"Good. But let's talk about that later," Ly suggested, moving closer, making me understand the heat in his eyes as his tongue moved out to lick the corner of his mouth, showing me the fork that told me all I needed to know.

The heat bloomed through my core, spreading immediately, making the need course through my entire body.

"What do you want to talk about now?" I asked, head tilting to the side, teasing, playing innocent.

"I want to talk about my cock in your pussy," he said, moving closer, hand grabbing my skirt, yanking it upward, and exposing me to the cool air. "Then maybe your ass," he added, grabbing me, turning me, pushing me forward against a tree.

One of his hands slapped my ass hard before I heard the zip of his pants.

There was no preamble.

He knew I was aching for him.

There was no need.

His cock slammed inside me—hard, deep—making me brace my arms on the tree trunk, shoving my ass back out toward him.

He fucked me the way we both knew I wanted it right then.

Hard.

Fast.

Driving me up and through an orgasm more quickly than ever before. Then giving me no rest as he drove me up again; this time, his thrusts slower, but powerful, my entire body jolting forward, my arms getting scraped up by the tree bark.

His hand moved between my thighs, toying with my clit, then moved between us, pressing against, then in, my ass, creating an even more intoxicating friction as he continued to fuck me.

"Tell me you want me to fuck your ass," he demanded.

"I want you to fuck my ass."

I hadn't had him that way yet.

I didn't even question it.

I just knew that every way I had him was amazing.

And I wanted whatever else he could give to me.

"Yeah, you do," he agreed, hand moving, cock slipping out of me, sliding it up and back, dripping with my wetness.

He was as slow and careful as he had been with my first time, pushing patiently inward, creating a familiar aching, pinching, that eased once he was settled deep, and his hand slid between my thighs, teasing over my clit. "Always so hungry for my cock," he rumbled as I rocked my hips back against him. "Here," he demanded, releasing my clit to grab my arm, yanking it down, pushing it between my thighs to start working myself in circles.

While his fingers thrust inside my pussy, turning, raking over the top wall while he began to fuck me, slow and easy at first, then building, going harder, faster, as we both got lost in the moment, as we drove upward together.

"Harder," I demanded, feeling the need reach that critical apex. "Ly, harder," I demanded, moaning as his free hand slapped hard on my ass as he gave me what I wanted, what I needed.

The orgasm crashed through me, making me cry out his name as he hissed out his release, leaning forward over me, his wrings wrapping me up, keeping me warm as he came back down.

"Fuck," he hissed a long moment later, sliding out of me.

"Yeah," I agreed, taking a deep breath as I straightened, pulling my skirt down again.

"A lifetime of that?" he said, tucking himself away. "Sign me up," he said, giving me a wicked smirk.

"Yeah, I think I brokered a good deal for myself," I agreed, smiling.

"Though, now we do have two new-to-Earth demons to deal with for the rest of that eternity too," he said, grimacing.

"Daemon seems like he is tolerable."

"Bael is going to be trouble."

"Well, luckily for us, you all love trouble," I said, shrugging.

"It will be an interesting eternity, I'll give you that," he agreed, wrapping an arm around me, pulling me into his side as we made our way back toward the house. "There's no one I'd rather spend it with," he added, pressing a kiss to my temple. "My witch," he added.

Yes, I'd gotten the best part of the deal.

Eternity.

With the man who my soul had decided was the one.

Epilogue

Lenore - 6 months

Ace deemed the "puppies" trained enough to take out of the house.

There was a biker meetup a couple of states over, something the men—and usually Red—went to every year, making new connections, selling product to continue to stock their coffers, inviting the next slew of humans to the house for a party. Where they would whisper in their ears, bring out their basest of instincts, slowly turn borderline souls evil, so their comrades in hell could have more souls to play around with.

There were some changes in me.

After all, that previous statement would have—before my deal—filled me with disgust and displeasure. Now, though, all I felt was an understanding.

Evil souls had to be punished.

Demons did that.

There was always a natural order to the world.

"When do I get my own motorcycle?" Daemon asked, hopping off the back of his brother's bike at the meet-up, seeing rows and rows of chrome and a sea of men and women to accompany them.

"When you can drive one without crashing it," Ace told him, rolling his eyes.

For all his teasing of Daemon, it was clear to me that Ace had a soft spot for him. Maybe he reminded him of a younger brother he'd left behind in hell.

As for Daemon's actual brother, Bael's general ornery and withdrawn demeanor hadn't softened at all yet. He didn't want to be stuck here. He made it clear he was just biding his time to get back. And since most of the others were in the same boat, they didn't fault him for his attitude.

That said, he had proven surprisingly adaptable, picking up on the human things like driving and use of electronics with relative ease.

He struggled where Daemon excelled, namely in all things that involved people or societal norms. Which was why he was in stony silence the whole day as the men moved around, making new connections, checking on old ones.

"Didn't realize your kind was recruiting," a familiar voice said as we passed.

I turned to find Sully standing there, eyeing Bael and Daemon for a moment before his gaze fell on me.

"What the fuck are you now?" he asked, body tensing.

"Off-limits," Ly said, tone low, lethal, eyes burning bright.

"Walk away," Ace demanded, gaze moving around, likely noting how many witnesses there would be to the event if Ly lost control of the Change, and his wings came flying out to protect me.

"They're going to be a problem again eventually," Seven observed as we got to the other side of the rally.

"Yeah, that's for another day," Ace agreed. "Shit. Here comes today's problem," he added, nodding his chin toward a woman who was making a beeline for our gathered group.

A woman I personally recognized as well.

From the party.

After my little public tryst with Ly.

When I was upset.

Short, fit, strong, and curvy.

Blonde-haired.

Green-eyed.

Dale.

The woman who'd almost referred to the men as demons before she caught herself.

"You!" she said, making a beeline for me, eyes enraged. "Oh," she said as she moved in front of me, shaking her head. "You stupid, stupid girl. What did you let them do to you?" she asked, voice seething. "Now I have to take you out too," she said, giving me one last hard look before marching away again, disappearing into the crowd in a blink.

"Lenore," Ace called, voice questioning, yet firm. "You know Dale?"

"I, ah, yeah. Who is she?" I asked, brows furrowing at her ominous message.

"Dale," Ace started, tone low, "is this generation's demonslayer. She kills us, or we kill her. Just like every other demonslayer. Where did you meet her? When you were in the coven? Are they working together against us?" he asked, strategic mind working in circles.

"I, ah, no. No. She was at your party," I told them, shrugging.

"Wait... what?" Seven asked, tensing. "You're sure?"

"I mean, yes. That's how she knows me. I was at the party."

Ace shot Ly a lifted brow, both of them acknowledging that he'd broken the rules, but also that it was too late for that now.

"How the fuck did she get in the house undetected?" Ace asked, waving out an arm.

"That's a great question. A really great question," Daemon said, bouncing a bit on his heels. "But there are a lot of women here. With a lot of mouths. And I was promised to be allowed to, oh what was the word? Charm them. I need to charm them onto their knees," he said, eyes dancing, shooting a boyish smirk my way. "I think I can manage that, right, Lenore?"

"I think you'll do fine, Daemon," I agreed. Ly grumbled.

The rest of the day was similar to the beginning. A lot of connections, a lot of talking. And, for me, a lot of standing around, thinking. Mostly about Dale. About her disappointment in me. About her vow to take me out.

"Ly, I thought you were immortal," I said later at the motel, pulling my clothes back on.

"*We* are," he corrected.

"Then why was Ace scared of Dale? Why did Dale say she could take me, and us, out?"

"Because, *she* can. She's the only one who can. Much like we're infused with the blood of the devil, she is infused with the blood of the Almighty. We're pure evil. She's pure good. And she is the only one with the power to end us."

"But... wouldn't you go back to hell?"

"No. She erases us entirely. Relax," he told me, his wing moving out to embrace me. "We've known half a dozen demonslayers. We are all still standing. None of them are. It will be fine. We will be fine," he said, pressing a quick kiss to my lips. "I am going to jump in the shower. Can you watch for the food?"

"Yep," I agreed, giving him a smile as I dipped into his wallet, grabbing the cash, then moving out onto the covered porch that connected all the motel rooms.

All the rooms on each side were occupied by the others. Ace, Drex, Seven, Bael, Daemon—who, from the sounds of things, had a whole harem of happy women in his room with him—and...

Even as I was about to think his name, the door to Minos's room opened.

But instead of Minos emerging, it was a woman.

A very familiar woman.

With sex-mussed hair and pink cheeks, still pulling her shirt down to cover her body.

"Don't," Dale said, looking over at me, eyes going hard. "Don't you dare judge me after what you've done," she said.

"Minos?" I asked, the pieces starting to fall together.

"I break real, human men," she said, jaw tight. "And we all need release. That's all it is," she insisted before running off, jumping on her own bike, and peeling out.

My head turned, finding Minos standing in his doorway, his gaze following the disappearing bike.

His wings were out.

"Oh, Minos," I said, my heart aching in my chest as he turned, letting me see his tortured gaze.

That was why she'd been at the party.

To sleep with Minos. Because he was the only man she could know on a carnal level without seriously hurting—or killing—him.

That was why she rushed out without trying to kill any of the demons.

Because that was not why she was there.

"How?" I asked, as he tried to control the Change, the Claiming. But there was no use. He couldn't control it anymore than Lycus could. "How is that possible?"

"It's not supposed to be," he said, shaking his head. "She hates me," he added. "She needs me, but she hates me. And I can't fucking help myself."

"Oh, Minos. I'm so sorry."

"One day, she is going to kill me."

"Minos..."

"Or they will try to kill her, and have to go through me to do it. There's no good end to this."

"I don't know what to say," I admitted.

"For right now, can you say nothing?" he asked, eyes pleading with me. Even knowing the ugly fate ahead, he couldn't help it. He wanted her to keep showing up, to keep using him, to take what she needed and leave. Because his nature ached for any contact with her, no matter the outcome, and the pain after.

"I, ah, okay. For now," I added, knowing there might come a time when I had to say something.

"Thank you," he said, ducking quickly inside the door when mine opened behind me.

"Everything alright?" Ly asked, hair dripping onto the shoulder of his white shirt.

"Yeah, just thinking," I told him, giving him a smile.

"About?"

"Just that you were right."

"About what?" he asked, stepping out, and closing the door behind him.

"About how interesting our eternity is promising to be."

"That it will, witch, that it will," he agreed, coming up behind me, pressing a kiss to my neck.

XX

Acknowledgments

Super big thanks to my bestie, Crystalyn, for everything.

Sheri, my proofreader, for fitting me in last minute when I had this idea to work on this.

KC - for the blurb help, always.

My ARC gals. For being excited to give this a try with me. And for being the best cheerleaders a writer could ask for.

Also by Jessica Gadziala

The Henchmen MC
Reign
Cash
Wolf
Repo
Duke
Renny
Lazarus
Pagan
Cyrus
Edison
Reeve
Sugar
The Fall of V
Adler

THE SACRIFICE
Roderick
Virgin
Roan
Camden
West
Colson

The Savages
Monster
Killer
Savior

Mallick Brothers
For A Good Time, Call
Shane
Ryan
Mark
Eli
Charlie & Helen: Back to the Beginning

Investigators
367 Days
14 Weeks
4 Months

Dark
Dark Mysteries
Dark Secrets
Dark Horse

Professionals
The Fixer

The Ghost
The Messenger
The General
The Babysitter
The Middle Man
The Negotiator
The Client

Rivers Brothers
Lift You Up
Lock You Down
Pull You In

STANDALONES WITHIN NAVESINK BANK:
Vigilante
Grudge Match

NAVESINK BANK LEGACY SERIES:
The Rise of Ferryn
Counterfeit Love

OTHER SERIES AND STANDALONES:

Stars Landing
What The Heart Needs
What The Heart Wants
What The Heart Finds
What The Heart Knows
The Stars Landing Deviant
What The Heart Learns

Surrogate

THE SACRIFICE
The Sex Surrogate
Dr. Chase Hudson

The Green Series
Into the Green
Escape from the Green

DEBT
Dissent
Stuffed: A Thanksgiving Romance
Unwrapped
Peace, Love, & Macarons
A Navesink Bank Christmas
Don't Come
Fix It Up
N.Y.E.
faire l'amour
Revenge
There Better Be Pie
The Woman in the Trunk

About the Author

Jessica Gadziala is a full-time writer, parrot enthusiast, and coffee drinker who has an unhealthy obsession with acquiring houseplants. She enjoys short rides to the book store, sad songs, and cold weather. She lives in New Jersey with her parrots, dogs, and a whole flock of chickens.

She is very active on Goodreads, Facebook, as well as her personal groups on those sites. Join in. She's friendly.

Stalk Her!

Connect with Jessica:

Facebook:
https://www.facebook.com/JessicaGadziala/
Facebook Group:
https://www.facebook.com/groups/314540025563403/

Goodreads:
https://www.goodreads.com/author/show/13800950.Jessica_Gadziala
Goodreads Group:
https://www.goodreads.com/group/show/177944-jessica-gadziala-books-and-bullsh

Twitter: @JessicaGadziala

JessicaGadziala.com

<3/ Jessica